This Book Belongs to:

My name is _HUNTER_

I am _4_ years old.

My parent(s) names are _MOM, DAD_

_____

My address is _3257_

_____

My telephone number is _32753_

TEACHER APPROVED!

Get Ready For
First Grade

280 ACTIVITIES AND 2,074 ILLUSTRATIONS

BLACK DOG
& LEVENTHAL
PUBLISHERS
NEW YORK

ISBN 978-1-57912-869-2

Library of Congress Cataloging-in-Publication Data on file
at the offices of Black Dog & Leventhal Publishers, Inc.

Manufactured in China

Published by
Black Dog & Leventhal Publishers, Inc.
151 West 19th Street
New York, New York 10011

Distributed by
Workman Publishing Company
225 Varick Street
New York, New York 10014

h g f e d c b

Contents

7   A Note to Parents

9   The Alphabet

65   Consonants

77   Vowels

109   Word Games

131   Numbers & Counting

173   Addition & Subtraction

213   Colors

225   Shapes

241   Opposties

245   Our World

308   Answers

317   Suggested Reading List

A Note to Parents

Get Ready for First Grade is an indispensable educational companion for your kindergarten child. It is chock full of fun, interesting, curriculum-based activities—such as those focusing on the alphabet, numbers, colors, shapes, math, nature, and more— that will introduce your child to new concepts while reinforcing what he or she already knows. In addition, there are plenty of fun word games, mazes, coloring activities, and crafts that are designed to entertain and amuse your child while boosting his or her basic skills.

In the back of the book you will find answers to some of the more difficult exercises and a Suggested Reading List. We recommend setting aside some time each day to read with your child. The more your child reads, the faster he or she will acquire other skills. We also suggest that you work with your child to complete a portion of the book each day. You can sit down together and discuss what the goals for each day will be, and perhaps even choose a reward to be given upon completion of the whole book—such as a trip to the park, a special play date, or something else that seems appropriate to you. While you want to help your child set educational goals, be sure to offer lots of encouragement along the way. These activities are not meant as a test. By making them fun and rewarding, you will help your child look forward to completing them, and he or she will be especially eager to tackle the educational challenges ahead! ★

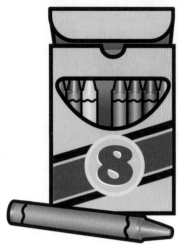

Hey Kids!
Remember to have
a pencil and
some crayons
handy when
playing with your
Get Ready book!

Start here...

FROM A TO Z

The Alphabet

...End here

The Alphabet

Aa Bb Cc Dd

Ee Ff Gg Hh

Ii Jj Kk Ll Mm

Nn Oo Pp Qq

Rr Ss Tt Uu Vv

Ww Xx Yy Zz

The Alphabet Game

Point to each letter of the alphabet on the opposite page and say it out loud. Now point to an object on this page and say its name. What letter of the alphabet does it start with? Find the letter. Do this with each thing on this page. You know your letters!

The big letter

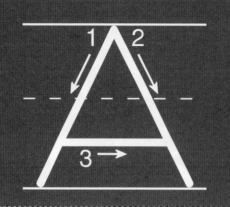

Apple

This is the uppercase letter **A**. Use your finger to trace it.
Now practice writing the uppercase letter **A** by following the arrows.

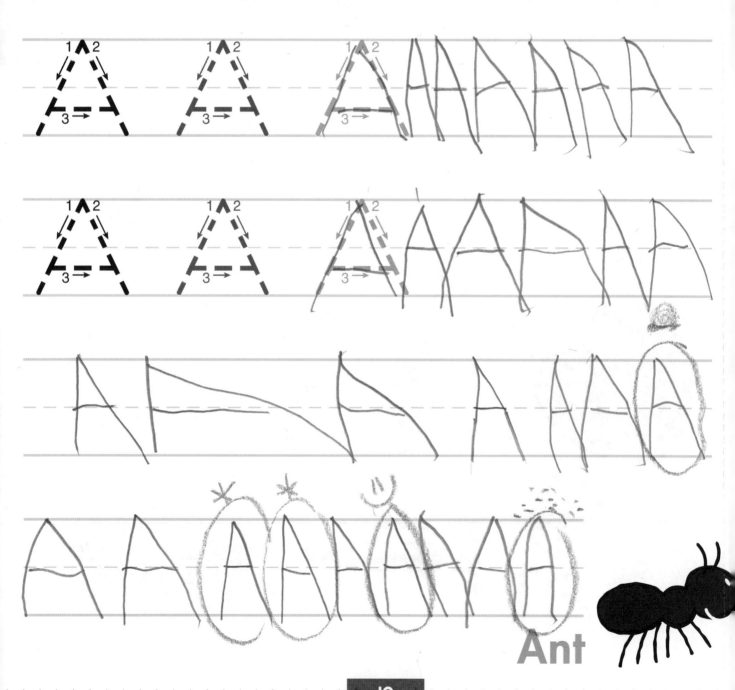

Ant

The little letter

airplane

This is the lowercase letter **a**. Use your finger to trace it.
Now practice writing the lowercase letter **a** by following the arrows.

Say out loud some words that begin with the letter **A**.

The big letter

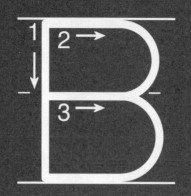

Ball

This is the uppercase letter **B**. Use your finger to trace it.
Now practice writing the uppercase letter **B** by following the arrows.

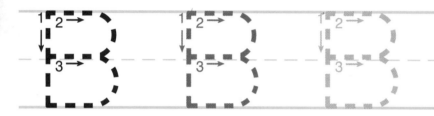

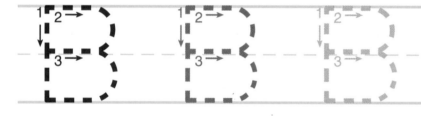

Ballerina

The little letter

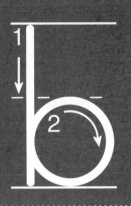

banana

This is the lowercase letter **b**. Use your finger to trace it.
Now practice writing the lowercase letter **b** by following the arrows.

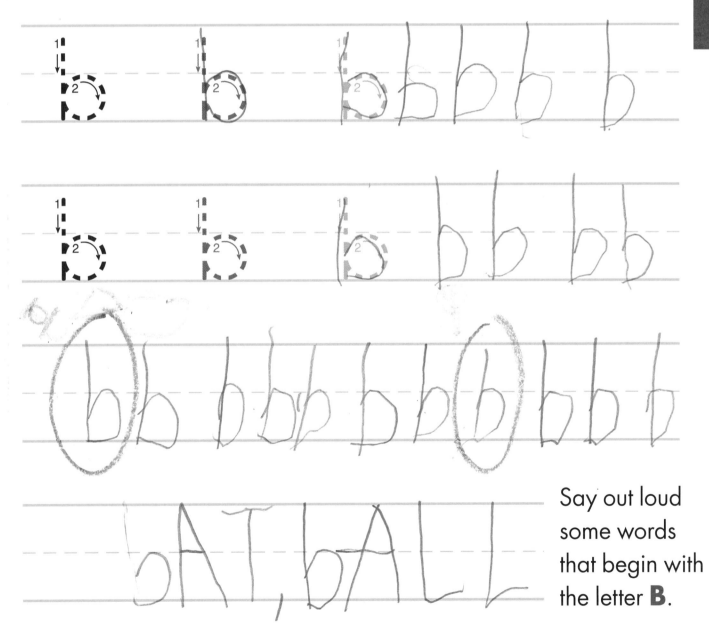

Say out loud some words that begin with the letter **B**.

The big letter

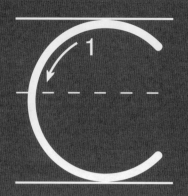

Cake

This is the uppercase letter **C**. Use your finger to trace it.
Now practice writing the uppercase letter **C** by following the arrows.

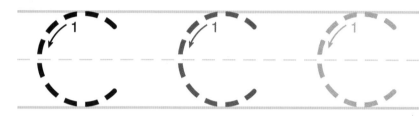

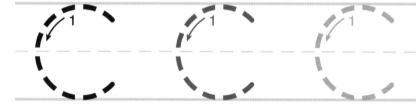

Cat

The little letter

can

This is the lowercase letter **c**. Use your finger to trace it.
Now practice writing the lowercase letter **c** by following the arrows.

Say out loud some words that begin with the letter **C**.

The big letter D

Dog

This is the uppercase letter **D**. Use your finger to trace it.
Now practice writing the uppercase letter **D** by following the arrows.

Doll

The little letter

 **duck**

This is the lowercase letter **d**. Use your finger to trace it.
Now practice writing the lowercase letter **d** by following the arrows.

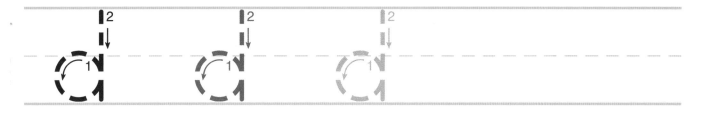

Say out loud some words that begin with the letter **D**.

The big letter

Elephant

This is the uppercase letter **E**. Use your finger to trace it.
Now practice writing the uppercase letter **E** by following the arrows.

Eggs

The little letter

elbow

This is the lowercase letter **e**. Use your finger to trace it.
Now practice writing the lowercase letter **e** by following the arrows.

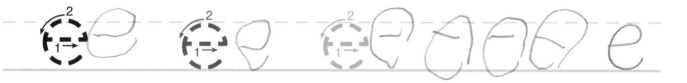

Say out loud some words that begin with the letter **E**.

The big letter

Fish

This is the uppercase letter **F**. Use your finger to trace it.
Now practice writing the uppercase letter **F** by following the arrows.

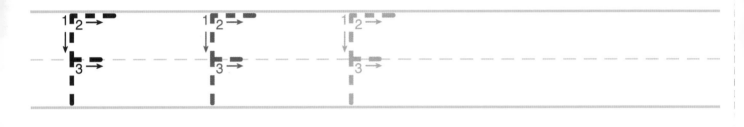

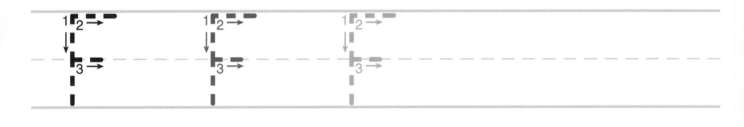

Firetruck

The little letter

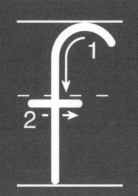

fairy

This is the lowercase letter **f**. Use your finger to trace it.
Now practice writing the lowercase letter **f** by following the arrows.

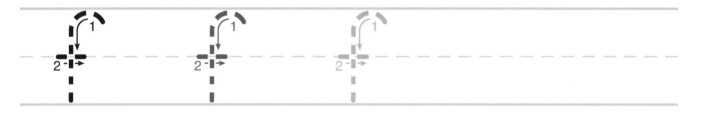

Say out loud some words that begin with the letter **F**.

The big letter

This is the uppercase letter **G**. Use your finger to trace it.
Now practice writing the uppercase letter **G** by following the arrows.

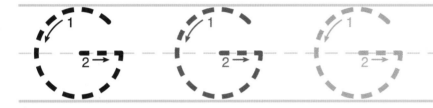

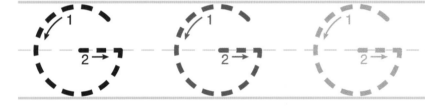

Guitar

The little letter g

grapes

This is the lowercase letter **g**. Use your finger to trace it.
Now practice writing the lowercase letter **g** by following the arrows.

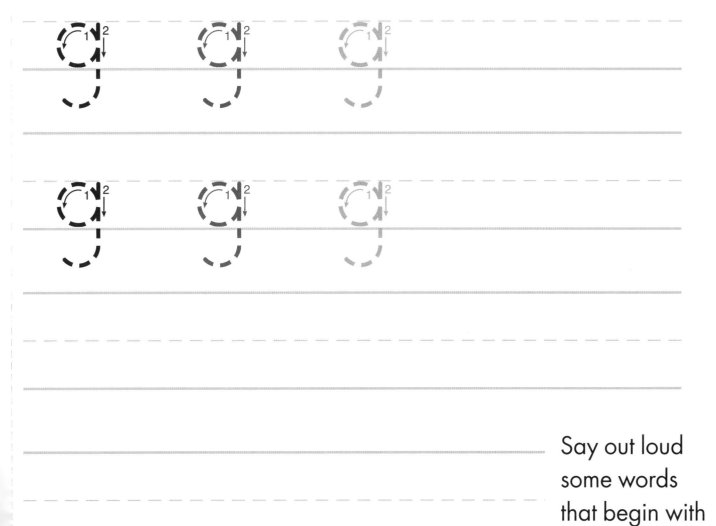

Say out loud some words that begin with the letter **G**.

The big letter

Hat

This is the uppercase letter **H**. Use your finger to trace it.
Now practice writing the uppercase letter **H** by following the arrows.

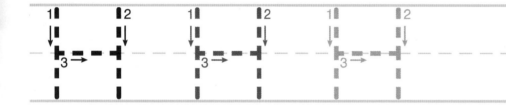

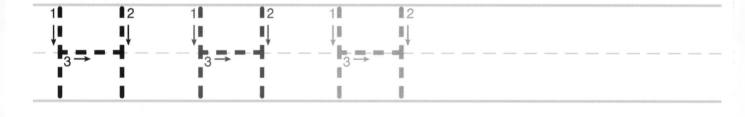

Heart

The little letter  hammer

This is the lowercase letter **h**. Use your finger to trace it.
Now practice writing the lowercase letter **h** by following the arrows.

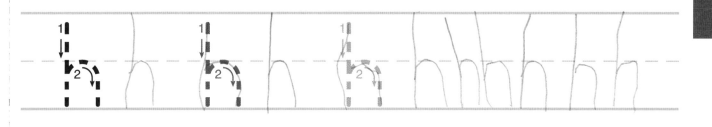

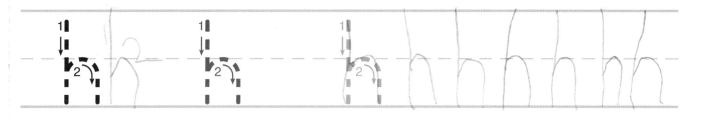

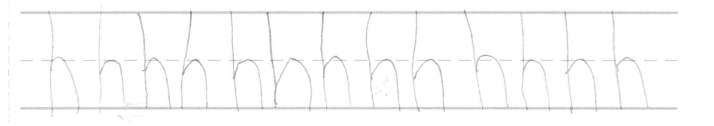

Say out loud some words that begin with the letter **H**.

The big letter

Igloo

This is the uppercase letter I. Use your finger to trace it.
Now practice writing the uppercase letter I by following the arrows.

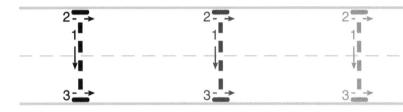

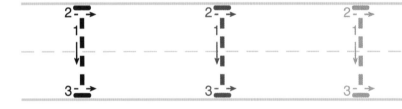

Ice cream

The little letter

insect

This is the lowercase letter **i**. Use your finger to trace it.
Now practice writing the lowercase letter **i** by following the arrows.

Say out loud some words that begin with the letter **I**.

The big letter

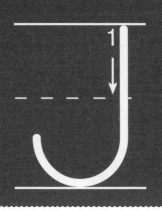

Jeans

This is the uppercase letter **J**. Use your finger to trace it.
Now practice writing the uppercase letter **J** by following the arrows.

Juicebox

The little letter j

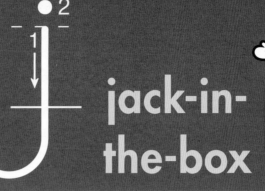 

jack-in-the-box

This is the lowercase letter **j**. Use your finger to trace it.
Now practice writing the lowercase letter **j** by following the arrows.

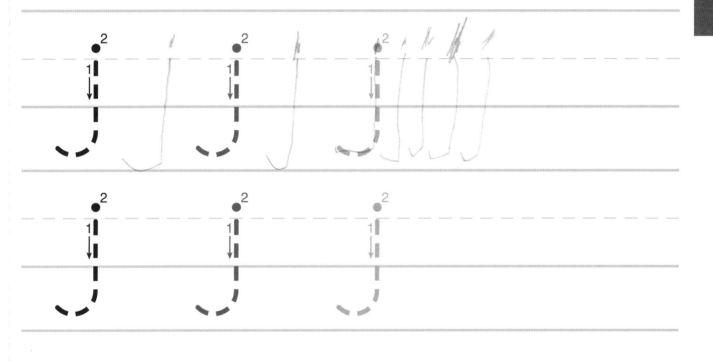

Say out loud some words that begin with the letter **J**.

The big letter

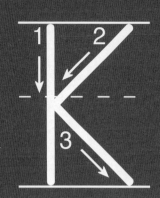

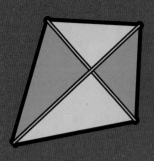

This is the uppercase letter **K**. Use your finger to trace it.
Now practice writing the uppercase letter **K** by following the arrows.

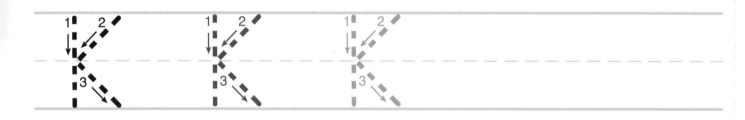

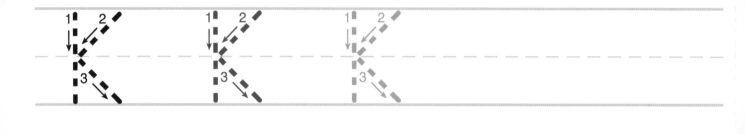

Kitten

The little letter

koala

This is the lowercase letter **k**. Use your finger to trace it.
Now practice writing the lowercase letter **k** by following the arrows.

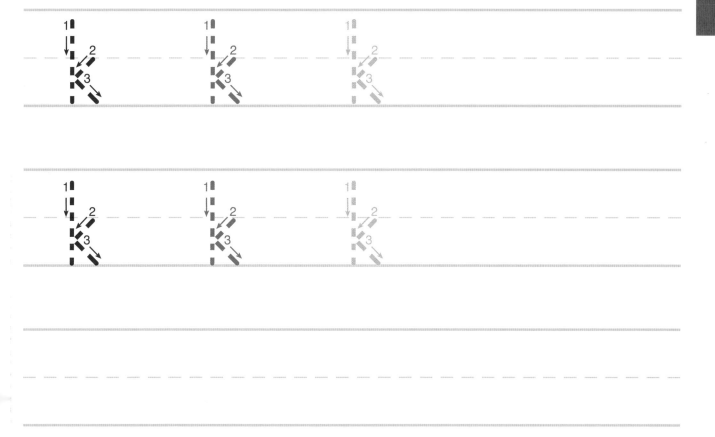

Say out loud some words that begin with the letter **K**.

The big letter

Lion

This is the uppercase letter **L**. Use your finger to trace it.
Now practice writing the uppercase letter **L** by following the arrows.

Ladybug

The little letter

lollipop

This is the lowercase letter l. Use your finger to trace it.
Now practice writing the lowercase letter l by following the arrows.

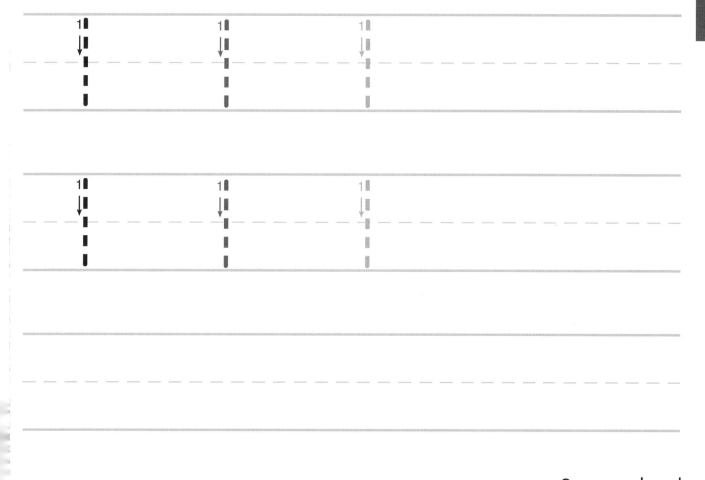

Say out loud some words that begin with the letter L.

The big letter M

Monkey

This is the uppercase letter **M**. Use your finger to trace it.
Now practice writing the uppercase letter **M** by following the arrows.

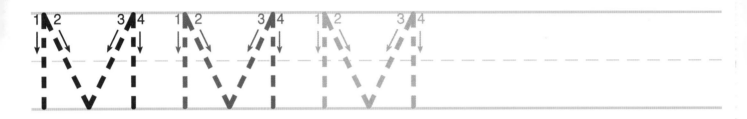

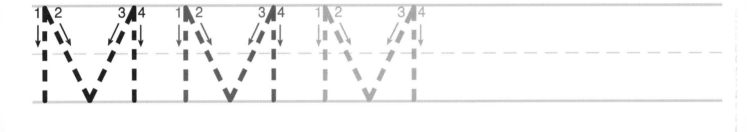

Motorcycle

The little letter

moon

This is the lowercase letter **m**. Use your finger to trace it.
Now practice writing the lowercase letter **m** by following the arrows.

Say out loud some words that begin with the letter **M**.

The big letter

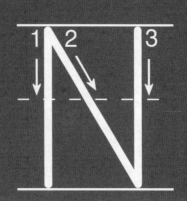

Nest

This is the uppercase letter **N**. Use your finger to trace it.
Now practice writing the uppercase letter **N** by following the arrows.

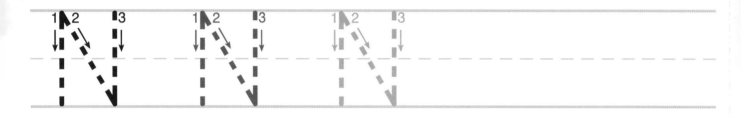

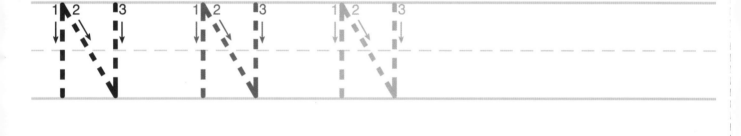

Necklace

The little letter

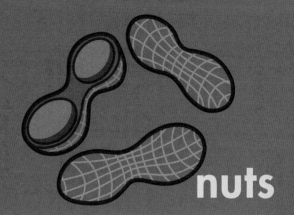

nuts

This is the lowercase letter **n**. Use your finger to trace it.
Now practice writing the lowercase letter **n** by following the arrows.

Say out loud
some words
that begin with
the letter **N**.

The big letter

This is the uppercase letter **O**. Use your finger to trace it.
Now practice writing the uppercase letter **O** by following the arrows.

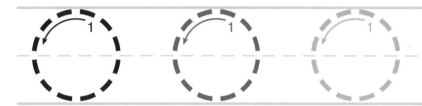

Owl

The little letter

ostrich

This is the lowercase letter **o**. Use your finger to trace it.
Now practice writing the lowercase letter **o** by following the arrows.

Say out loud some words that begin with the letter **O**.

The big letter

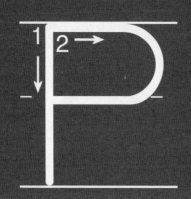

Panda

This is the uppercase letter **P**. Use your finger to trace it.
Now practice writing the uppercase letter **P** by following the arrows.

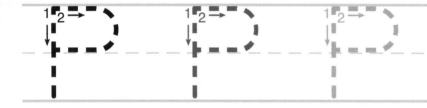

Pear

The little letter

phone

This is the lowercase letter **p**. Use your finger to trace it.
Now practice writing the lowercase letter **p** by following the arrows.

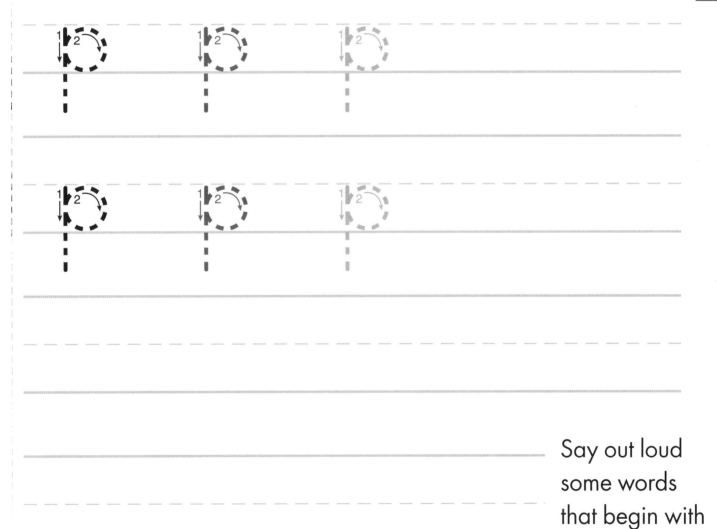

Say out loud some words that begin with the letter **P**.

The big letter

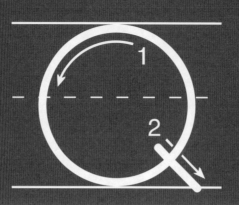

This is the uppercase letter **Q**. Use your finger to trace it.

Now practice writing the uppercase letter **Q** by following the arrows.

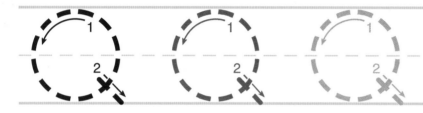

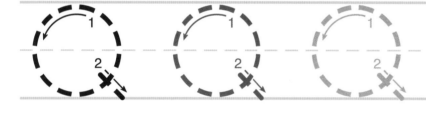

Queen

The little letter q

quail

This is the lowercase letter **q**. Use your finger to trace it.
Now practice writing the lowercase letter **q** by following the arrows.

Say out loud some words that begin with the letter **Q**.

The big letter

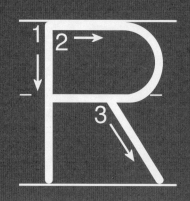

Robot

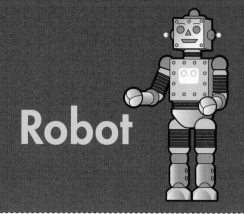

This is the uppercase letter **R**. Use your finger to trace it.
Now practice writing the uppercase letter **R** by following the arrows.

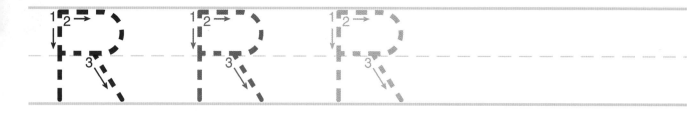

Rainbow

The little letter

rooster

This is the lowercase letter **r**. Use your finger to trace it.
Now practice writing the lowercase letter **r** by following the arrows.

Say out loud some words that begin with the letter **R**.

The big letter

This is the uppercase letter **S**. Use your finger to trace it.
Now practice writing the uppercase letter **S** by following the arrows.

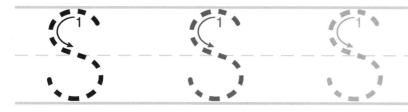

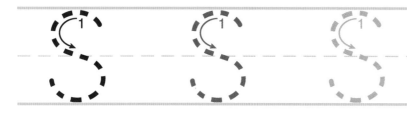

Spider

The little letter s

sailboat

This is the lowercase letter **s**. Use your finger to trace it.
Now practice writing the lowercase letter **s** by following the arrows.

Say out loud some words that begin with the letter **S**.

The big letter

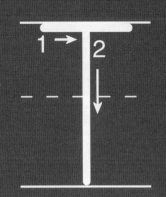

Turtle

This is the uppercase letter **T**. Use your finger to trace it.
Now practice writing the uppercase letter **T** by following the arrows.

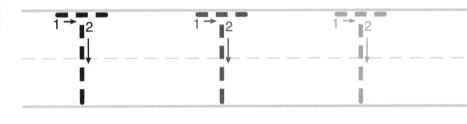

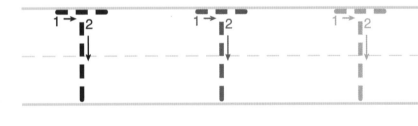

Tree

The little letter

truck

This is the lowercase letter **t**. Use your finger to trace it.
Now practice writing the lowercase letter **t** by following the arrows.

Say out loud some words that begin with the letter **T**.

The big letter

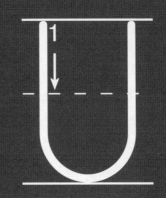

This is the uppercase letter **U**. Use your finger to trace it.
Now practice writing the uppercase letter **u** by following the arrows.

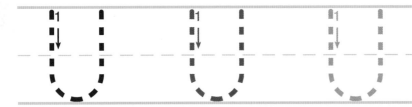

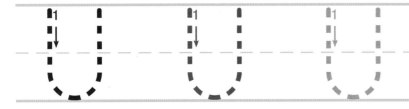

Umbrella

The little letter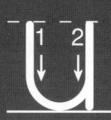

14 uniform

This is the lowercase letter **u**. Use your finger to trace it.
Now practice writing the lowercase letter **u** by following the arrows.

Say out loud
some words
that begin with
the letter **U**.

The big letter

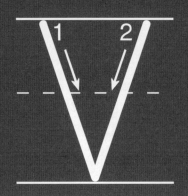

Violin

This is the uppercase letter **V**. Use your finger to trace it.
Now practice writing the uppercase letter **V** by following the arrows.

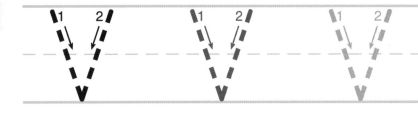

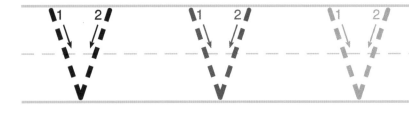

Vacuum

The little letter

vegetables

This is the lowercase letter **v**. Use your finger to trace it.
Now practice writing the lowercase letter **v** by following the arrows.

Say out loud some words that begin with the letter **V**.

The big letter

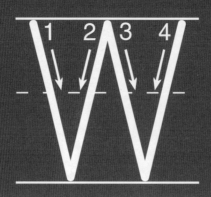

Whale

This is the uppercase letter **W**. Use your finger to trace it.
Now practice writing the uppercase letter **W** by following the arrows.

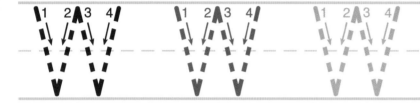

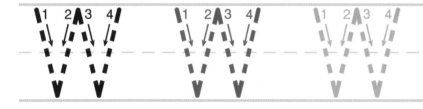

Wagon

The   watermelon

This is the lowercase letter **w**. Use your finger to trace it.
Now practice writing the lowercase letter **w** by following the arrows

Say out loud some words that begin with the letter **W**.

The big letter

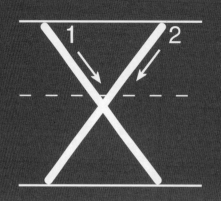

This is the uppercase letter **X**. Use your finger to trace it.

Now practice writing the uppercase letter **X** by following the arrows.

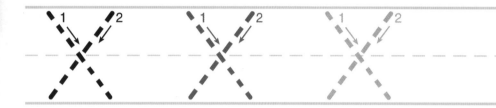

The little letter

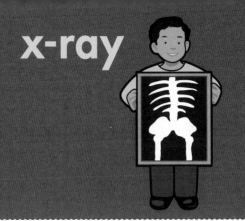

This is the lowercase letter **x**. Use your finger to trace it.
Now practice writing the lowercase letter **x** by following the arrows.

Say out loud
some words
that begin with
the letter **X**.

The big letter

This is the uppercase letter **Y**. Use your finger to trace it.
Now practice writing the uppercase letter **Y** by following the arrows.

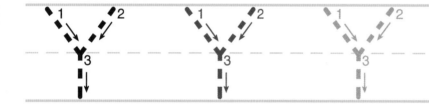

Yarn

The little letter

y yogurt

This is the lowercase letter **y**. Use your finger to trace it.
Now practice writing the lowercase letter **y** by following the arrows.

Say out loud some words that begin with the letter **Y**.

The big letter

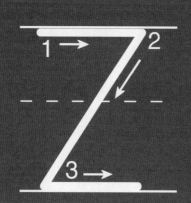

Zebra

This is the uppercase letter **Z**. Use your finger to trace it.
Now practice writing the uppercase letter **Z** by following the arrows.

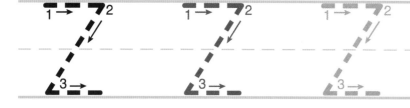

Zipper

The little letter

ZOO

This is the lowercase letter **z**. Use your finger to trace it.
Now practice writing the lowercase letter **z** by following the arrows.

Say out loud some words that begin with the letter **Z**.

Let's Review

Now, say the whole alphabet out loud.

A a B b C c D d
E e F f G g H h
I i J j K k L l M m
N n O o P p Q q
R r S s T t U u V v
W w X x Y y Z z

Consonants

CONSONANTS

Consonants are all of the letters in the alphabet that aren't vowels. Circle the consonants in the following words.

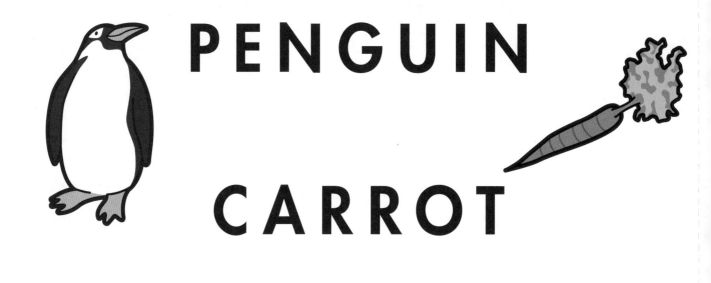

PENGUIN

CARROT

JACKET

SHOVEL

Consonants
B C D

Come up with as many words as you can that begin with the consonants **B**, **C**, and **D**, and write them on the lines below.

B **baseball** _____ _____

_____ _____ _____

C _____ _____ _____

_____ _____ _____

D _____ _____ _____

_____ _____ _____

Consonants

Consonants
F G H

Come up with as many words as you can that begin with the consonants **F**, **G**, and **H**, and write them on the lines below.

F fish _____ _____

_____ _____ _____

G _____ _____ _____

_____ _____ _____

H _____ _____ _____

_____ _____ _____

Consonants
J K L

Come up with as many words as you can that begin with the consonants **J**, **K**, and **L**, and write them on the lines below.

J jacket _____ _____

_____ _____ _____

K _____ _____ _____

_____ _____ _____

L _____ _____ _____

_____ _____ _____

Consonants
M N P

Come up with as many words as you can that begin with
the consonants **M**, **N**, and **P**, and write them on the lines below.

M mitten _____ _____

_____ _____ _____

N _____ _____ _____

_____ _____ _____

P _____ _____ _____

_____ _____ _____

Consonants
Q R S

Come up with as many words as you can that begin with the consonants **Q**, **R**, and **S**, and write them on the lines below.

Q quick _____ _____

_____ _____ _____

R _____ _____ _____

_____ _____ _____

S _____ _____ _____

_____ _____ _____

Consonants
T V W

Come up with as many words as you can that begin with the consonants **T**, **V**, and **W**, and write them on the lines below.

T tree _____ _____

_____ _____ _____

V _____ _____ _____

_____ _____ _____

W _____ _____ _____

_____ _____ _____

Consonants
X Y Z

Come up with as many words as you can that begin with the consonants **X**, **Y**, and **Z**, and write them on the lines below.

X x-ray _____ _____

_____ _____ _____

Y _____ _____ _____

_____ _____ _____

Z _____ _____ _____

_____ _____ _____

Consonants

Missing Consonants

Finish spelling the words below by filling in the correct consonants. Then color the pictures any way you like.

r a _ _ i t

c _ w

l a _ y _ u _

t a _ _ e

Missing Consonants

Finish spelling the words below by filling in the correct consonants.
Then color the pictures any way you like.

boa_t_ ✓

pea_R ✓

ki_t_t_e_N s_k_a_t_e_

SKATES

Missing Consonants

Finish spelling the words below by filling in the correct consonants.

looe

c L o w N

di N o s a u R

p L a N e

a L L i g a t o R

Vowels

Learn the Vowels

Almost every single word in English has a vowel in it. There are five vowels and each one has its own sound. The vowels are:

A

E

I

O

U

Say them out loud and then we can begin to learn how they are used in making up different words.

VOWELS

Copy down the five vowels here. Under each vowel come up with three words that begin with a vowel. The first one is done for you.

A___   E___   I___

ant

apple

airplane

O___   U___

The Long Vowel "a"

Vowels can be long or short. Long vowels sound just like the letter as you say it out loud. For example, the vowel **a** in the word bake sounds just like the letter **a**. Practice sounding out and reading these **long a** words.

bake

skates

gate

cake

date

cape

ape

table

Try to come up with some other words that have the **long a** sound.

The Short Vowel "a"

Vowels can be long or short.
For example, the vowel **a** in the word cat is a **short a**.
Practice sounding out and reading these **short a** words.

cat

van

fan

bat

man

hat

ham

map

Try to come up with some other words that have the **short a** sound.

The Long Vowel "e"

Practice sounding out and reading these **long e** words.

eel

tree

key

freeze

feel

sheep

zebra

sweet

Try to come up with some other words that have the **long e** sound.

The Short Vowel "e"

Practice sounding out and reading these **short e** words.

net

bed

hen

nest

pen

help

jet

mess

Try to come up with some other words that have the **short e** sound.

The Long Vowel "i"

Practice sounding out and reading these **long i** words.

pie
ice
wide
life
bike
pipe
tiger
rise

Try to come up with some other words that have the **long i** sound.

The Short Vowel "i"

Practice sounding out and reading these **short i** words.

bib

gift

hill

pig

fit

lip

fish

rip

Try to come up with some other words that have the **short i** sound.

The Long Vowel "o"

Practice sounding out and reading these **long o** words.

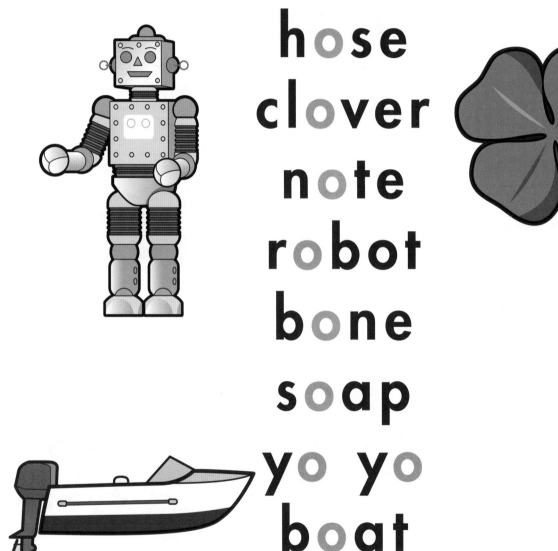

hose
clover
note
robot
bone
soap
yo yo
boat

Try to come up with some other words that have the **long o** sound.

The Short Vowel "o"

Practice sounding out and reading these **short o** words.

top
frog
clock
socks
mop
dog
fox

Try to come up with some other words that have the **short o** sound.

The Long Vowel "u"

Practice sounding out and reading these **long u** words.

cute

blue

cube

glue

tuba

fuel

fruit

juice

Try and come up with some other words that have the **long u** sound.

The Short Vowel "u"

Practice sounding out and reading these **short u** words.

bu**s**

su**n**

lu**ck**

fu**n**

ru**g**

du**ck**

cu**b**

mu**g**

Try to come up with some other words that have the **short u** sound.

The Long and Short Vowel "y"

Sometimes **Y** is a vowel, too.
Practice sounding out and reading these words where **Y** is a vowel.

tricycle
fly
gym
type
french fry
cry
eye

Try to come up with some other words where **y** is a vowel.

The Vowel "y" sounding like "e"

The vowel **Y** sometimes sounds like a long **E**. Practice sounding out and reading words where **Y** sounds like an **E**.

puppy
candy
fancy
chimney
handy
study
funny

Try to come up with some other words where **y** sounds like a long **e**.

Vowel Combinations

Words are spelled by combining vowels and other letters in specific combinations to make certain sounds, like those listed below. Say these vowel combinations out loud and read the words that use them.

ow / ou — owl, house

oo — book, balloon

oy / oi — toy, soil

or / ore / oar — cord, store, board

aw / au — fawn, autumn

ar /ir / ur / er — shark, bird, turtle, farmer

ear / eer — bear, deer

Fill in the missing letters with either **oy** or **oi**
to finish spelling the following words:

t _ _ l e t

t _ _

Vowels

Vowel Combinations
OW / OU

Fill in the missing letters with either **ow** or **ou** to finish spelling the following words:

h _ _ s e

_ _ l

Vowel Combinations
oo

Fill in the missing letters with **oo**
to finish spelling the following words:

b _ _ k

ball _ _ n

Vowel Combinations
aw / au

Fill in the missing letters with either **aw** or **au**
to finish spelling the following words:

f _ _ n

_ _ t u m n

Vowel Combinations
ar / ir / ur / er

Fill in the missing letters with either **ar**, **ir**, **ur**, or **er** to finish spelling the following words:

t _ _ t l e

b _ _ d

f a r m _ _

s h _ _ k

Missing Vowels

Look carefully at the pictures and write in the missing vowels.
Remember, the vowels are: **A E I O U**

t r _ ck

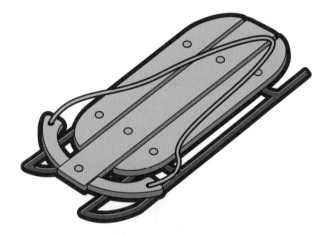

s l _ d

f _ sh

m _ l k

Missing Vowels

Look at the picture and write in the missing vowels.

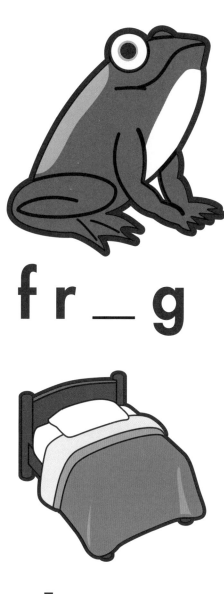

f r _ g

z _ b r a

b _ d

l _ o n

Vowel Combinations
ear / eer

All of the words below are missing either the letters **ear** or **eer**. Look at each word carefully and finish spelling it using these letter combinations.

b _ _ _

d _ _ _

Missing Vowels

Look at the picture and then write in the missing vowels.

f l _ w _ r

b _ _

g r _ p _ s

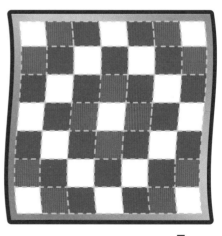

q _ _ l t

Missing Vowels

Look at the picture and then write in the missing vowels.

h _ r _

p _ _ r

w h _ l _

Missing Vowels

Write in the missing vowels
to finish spelling each word.

q u _ _ n

p _ _ n _ t

_ p p l _

ch _ ck _ n

Vowel Combinations
or / ore / oar

All of the words below are missing either the letters **or**, **ore**, or **oar**. Look at each word carefully and finish spelling it using one of these letter combinations.

c _ _ n

b _ _ _ d

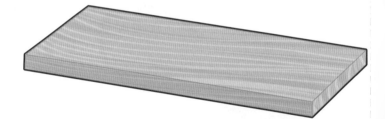

s c _ _ _

Missing Vowels

Finish spelling the words below by filling in the correct vowels.

b _ n _ n _   g _ _ t _ r

c _ s s _ r s   r _ b b _ n

Missing Vowels

Finish spelling the words below by filling in the correct vowels.

m _ p

_ r _ s _ r

g _ t _

s l _ d _

Missing Vowels

Finish spelling the words below by filling in the correct vowels.

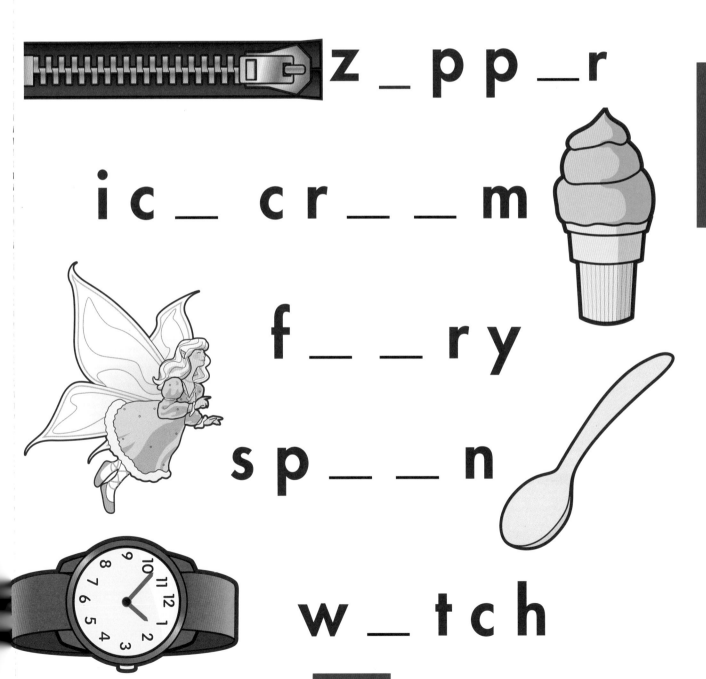

z _ p p _ r

i c _   c r _ _ m

f _ _ r y

s p _ _ n

w _ t c h

Let's Review Vowels

Can you remember all the vowels? Write them on the lines below.

_____   _____

_____

_____   _____

and sometimes

_____

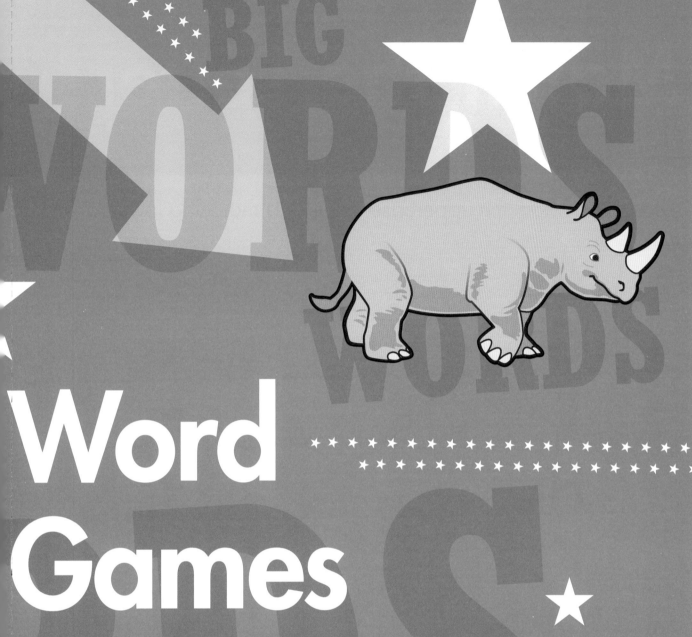

Word Games

Match the Letters

Draw a line from the uppercase letter to its matching lowercase.

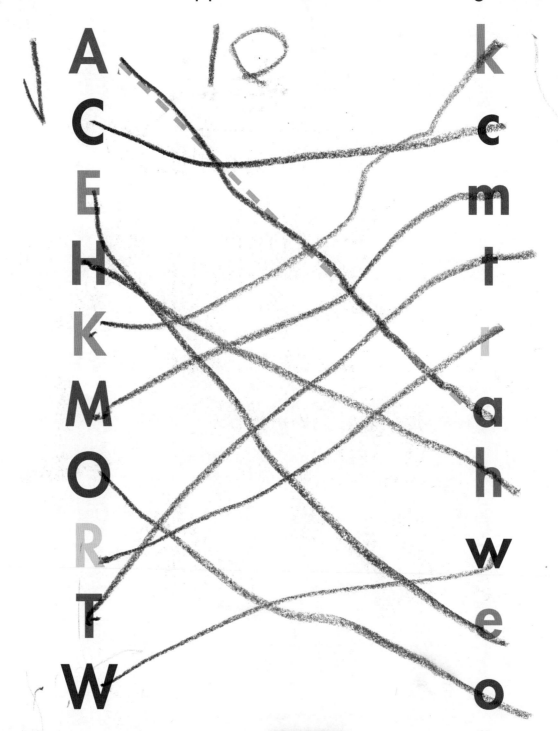

Connect the Letters

Start with the letter **A** and connect the letters to complete the drawing.
Color the picture when you have finished.

Word Games

Word Scramble
SEASONS

Unscramble the seasons: winter, spring, and autumn

_ _ _ _ _ _
M U T N A U

_ _ _ _ _ _
R E I W N T

_ _ _ _ _ _
P S G N R I

Word Scramble
RAINBOW

Unscramble the colors: red, purple, yellow, green, blue, and orange.

RED
EDR

PURPLE
PLERUP

LOLWEY

REGEN

BLUE
LUEB

ORANGE
GERANO

Word Games

What Rhymes With?

A rhyme is a word that sounds like another word but starts with a different letter, like hare and fair or coat and boat. Try to come up with words that rhyme with each of these words. Write the rhyming words in the blank spaces.

BYE FLY _____ _____ _____

BLOCK CLOCK _____ _____

DOOR STORE _____ _____

CAT BAT _____ _____

What Rhymes With?

Try to come up with words that rhyme with each of these words.
Write the rhyming words in the blank spaces.

BOX <u>FOX</u> _____ _____

TAP <u>MAP</u> _____ _____

HAIR <u>STARE</u> _____ _____

LATE <u>GREAT</u> _____ _____

Word Games

Word Scramble
SQUARE

Circle all of the letters you need to spell the word **SQUARE**.
Then write the word on the lines below, using lowercase letters.

A B I U S

D Q E R G

_ _ _ _ _ _

Word Scramble
RECTANGLE

Circle all of the letters you need to spell the word **RECTANGLE**.
Then write the word on the lines below, using lowercase letters.

T Q S R A D

G L C E N E

_ _ _ _ _ _ _ _ _

Word Scramble
OVAL

Circle all of the letters you need to spell the word **OVAL**.
Then write the word on the lines below, using lowercase letters.

B W V C A

T O X L Z

___ ___ ___ ___

Word Scramble
DIAMOND

Circle all of the letters you need to spell the word **DIAMOND**. Then write the word on the lines below, using lowercase letters.

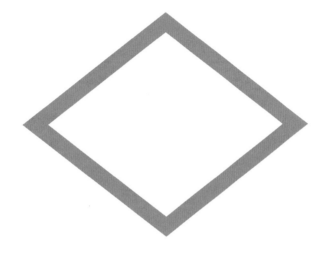

W A N M D

U O N T D I

_ _ _ _ _ _ _

Word Games

Word Scramble
FOOD

These scrambled words are all different foods that you eat.
Unscramble them and write their names on the lines.

AKEC __ __ __ __

MATTOO __ __ __ __ __ __

KECHNIC __ __ __ __ __ __ __

ROYGUT __ __ __ __ __ __

Word Scramble
ANIMALS

These scrambled words are animals at the zoo.
Unscramble them and write their names on the lines.

KYENMO __ __ __ __ __ __

OGRAOKNE __ __ __ __ __ __ __ __

GFRAIFE __ __ __ __ __ __ __

GETIR __ __ __ __ __

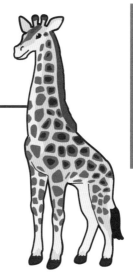

Let's Play with Letters

Look at the pictures carefully and say each word out loud.
Then write in the missing letters to spell the word.

s p _ d _ r

d _ _ m

p e _ _ _ i n

c l _ v _ r

Let's Play with Letters

Look at the pictures carefully and say each word out loud. Then write in the missing letters to spell the word.

s h _ _ t

g o _ t

r h _ n _

l _ _ p

Let's Play with Letters

Look at the pictures and then write in the missing letters to spell the word.
HINT: Each word is missing two of the **same** letters.

g o r i _ _ a   a _ _ l e

a _ _ _ i g a t o r

Let's Play with Letters

Look at the pictures and then write in the missing letters to spell the word.
HINT: Each word is missing two of the **same** letters.

s q u i r _ _

p a _ _ o t

Word Games

Let's Play with Letters

Look at the pictures carefully and say each word out loud.
Then write in the missing letters to spell the word.

n _ _ t

p _ _ t a

s t _ _ ll _ r

p _ p _ y

Let's Play with Letters

Look at the pictures carefully and say each word out loud.
Then write in the missing letters to spell the word.

b _ _ e   m _ _ t _ n s

v _ _ _ _ i n   m _ _ _ e

Word Games

The Sound of ch / sh

Circle the words below that **END** with **CH** or **SH**.

shell
catch
chicken
shrimp
crash
dish
trash
chimp
match

The Sound of th / wh

Circle the words below that **BEGIN** with **TH** or **WH**.

white

touch

thunder

wheel

three

thumb

whisper

whale

think

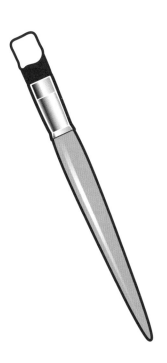

Word Games

Word Search

Read the words at the bottom of this page out loud. Each one is hidden in the grid below. Find each word and circle it. The words can be either across or down. The first one has been done for you.

```
D  A  K  C  H  I  C  K  E  Q
P  F  I  R  E  T  R  U  C  K
E  G  T  B  O  O  K  L  T  U
N  L  E  T  U  R  T  L  E  H
C  M  I  B  A  J  N  P  R  W
I  P  G  L  A  S  S  T  X  E
L  O  E  T  H  V  R  D  F  Y
A  K  M  J  E  E  P  C  I  T
R  D  F  T  L  N  E  A  B  S
C  I  G  K  Z  F  R  U  H  X
```

CHICK   BOOK   TURTLE   KITE
JEEP   GLASS   FIRETRUCK   PENCIL

IT'S AS EASY

Numbers & Counting

Count to TEN

Begin with zero and count to ten.

0 Clouds

1 Sun

2 Beach Balls

3 Shells

4 Buckets

5 Star fish

6 Shovels

7 Umbrellas

8 Fish

9 Towels

10 Sailboats

A Day at the Beach

Count how many of the objects appear
and write the number below.

 buckets  castles  balls

The Number 0 ZERO

This vase has **ZERO** flowers

This jar has **ZERO** pickles

Using a pencil follow the lines and make a perfect **0**.

The Number Zero

How many kids are sitting in this bus?

Answer: There are **0** kids sitting in this bus.
Practice drawing a zero on the lines below.

The Number 1   ONE

1 lemon

1 piggy bank

1 dragonfly

1 quilt

Using a pencil follow the lines and make a perfect **1**.
Then practice drawing the number **1** on a blank piece of paper.

1

The Number One

Color each picture that has **ONE** object in it.

2 helicoptors

2 motorcycles

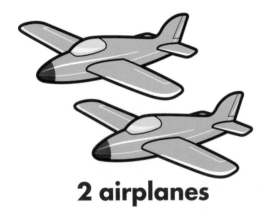

2 airplanes

2 trucks

Using a pencil follow the lines and make a perfect **2**.
Then practice drawing the number **2** on a blank piece of paper.

2 2 2 2 2

The Number Two

Color each picture when **TWO** appear.

The Number 3 THREE

3 hamburgers

3 pieces of pizza

3 ice cream cones

Using a pencil follow the lines and make a perfect **3**.
Then practice drawing the number **3** on a blank piece of paper.

The Number Three

Color each picture where **THREE** appear.

The Number 4 FOUR

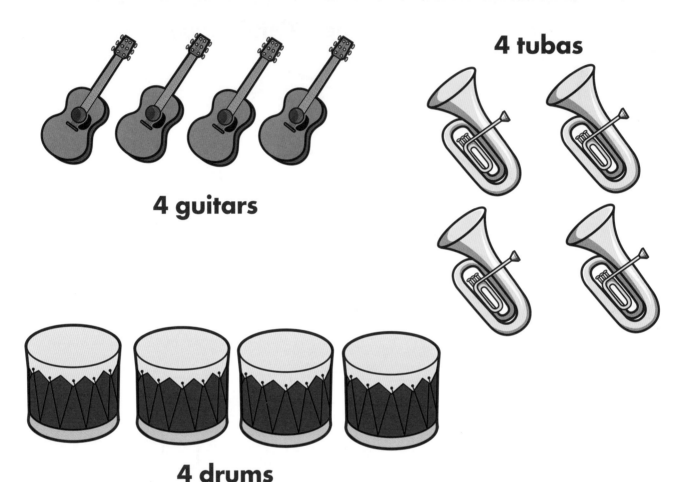

4 guitars

4 tubas

4 drums

Using a pencil follow the lines and make a perfect **4**.
Then practice drawing the number **4** on a blank piece of paper.

The Number Four

Color each picture where **FOUR** appear.

The Number 5   FIVE

5 butterflies

5 grasshoppers   **5 dragonflies**

Using a pencil follow the lines and make a perfect **5**.
Then practice drawing the number **5** on a blank piece of paper.

The Number Five

Color the **FIVE** insects hiding in the garden.

The Number 6 SIX

6 birds

6 eggs in a nest

6 trees

Using a pencil follow the lines and make a perfect **6**.
Then practice drawing the number **6** on a blank piece of paper.

The Number Six

Color the **SIX** birds in the tree.

The Number 7 SEVEN

7 rabbits

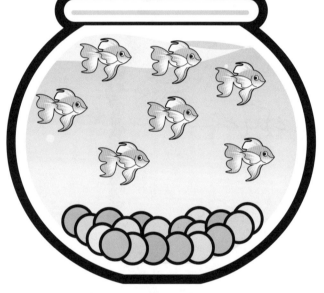

7 fish in a fishbowl

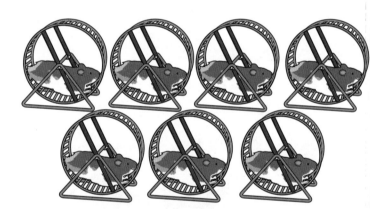

7 hampsters

Using a pencil follow the lines and make a perfect **7**.
Then practice drawing the number **7** on a blank piece of paper.

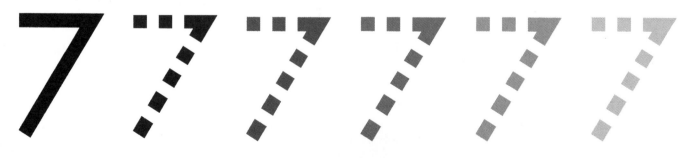

The Number Seven

Help the cat find her **SEVEN** kittens by coloring them.

The Number 8 EIGHT

8 zebra

8 arms of an octopus

8 monkey

Using a pencil follow the lines and make a perfect **8**.
Then practice drawing the number **8** on a blank piece of paper.

8 8 8 8 8 8

The Number Eight

Color the **EIGHT** animals in the zoo.

The Number 9 NINE

9 frogs

9 turtles

Using a pencil follow the lines and make a perfect **9**.
Then practice drawing the number **9** on a blank piece of paper.

9 9 9 9 9

The Number Nine

Color the **NINE** creatures in the pond.

The Number 10 TEN

10 party hats

10 candles on a cake

Using a pencil follow the lines and make a perfect **10**.
Then practice drawing the number **10** on a blank piece of paper.

10 10 10

The Number Ten

Color the **TEN** friends at the birthday party.

Connect the Dots

Complete the connect-the-dots by beginning at the number 1.
Color the picture when you are finished.

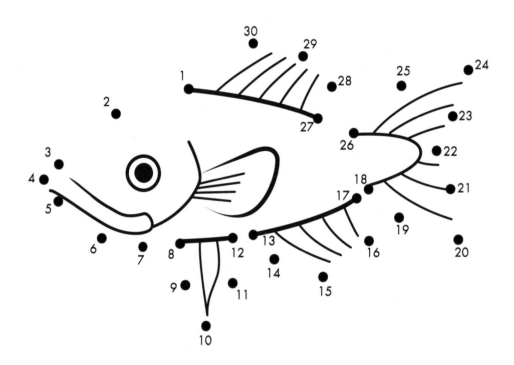

Connect the Dots

Find the dot with the number 2 and draw a line to connect all the dots, counting by 2s. Color the picture when you are finished.

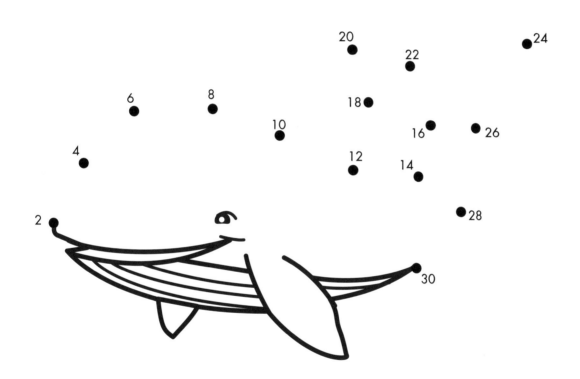

Count the Bubbles

Count the number of bubbles. Write the number below.

_____ **bubbles**

What's for Dinner?

How many items are in the refridgerator? Write the number below.

_9_ **items**

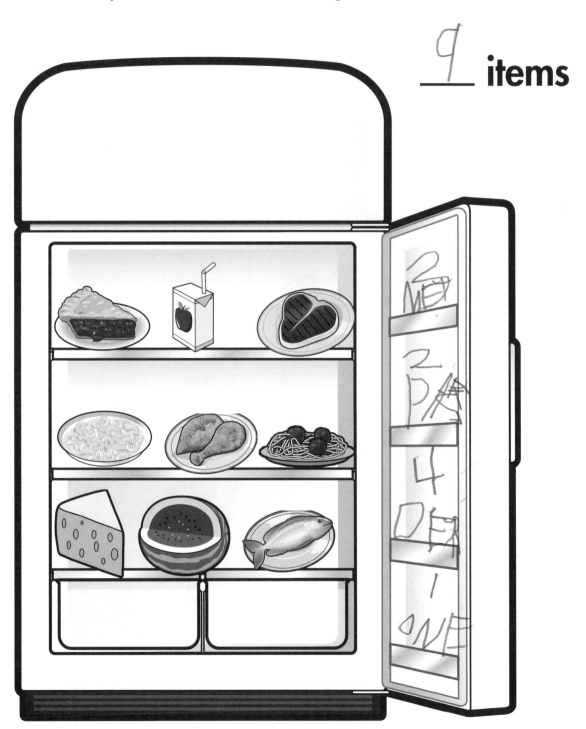

How Long?

How long is each caterpiller? Write the number of inches in the box.

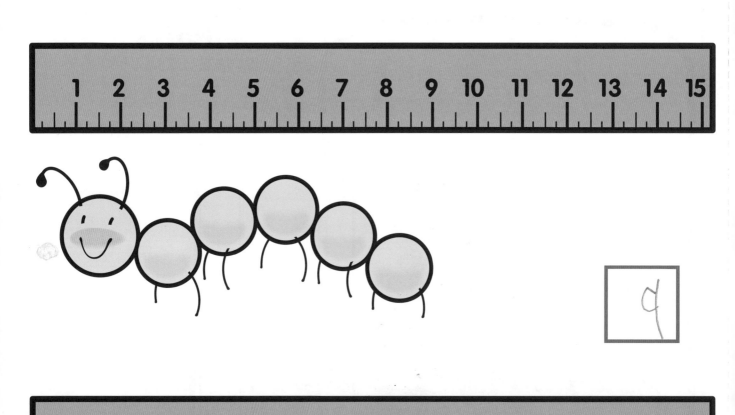

9

15

How Tall?

How tall is each animal? Write the number of inches in the box and color the animal that is the tallest.

Let's Count

Ladybugs are swarming! How many of each?
Write the correct answer below.

___ red
___ no spots
___ yellow
___ green

Let's Count Backwards

Now that you know how to count from one to ten
try counting backwards from 10 to 0.

10
9
8
7
6
5
4
3
2
1
0

How Many Are There?

Write the answers in the boxes.

How many **dolls** are in the house ?

How many **drawers** are in the bureau ?

How many **chairs** are in the kitchen ?

How many **windows** are there ?

How many **lamps** are in the house ?

How many **windowboxes** do you see ?

How Many Red?

Count the number of red squares in the quilt and write it below..

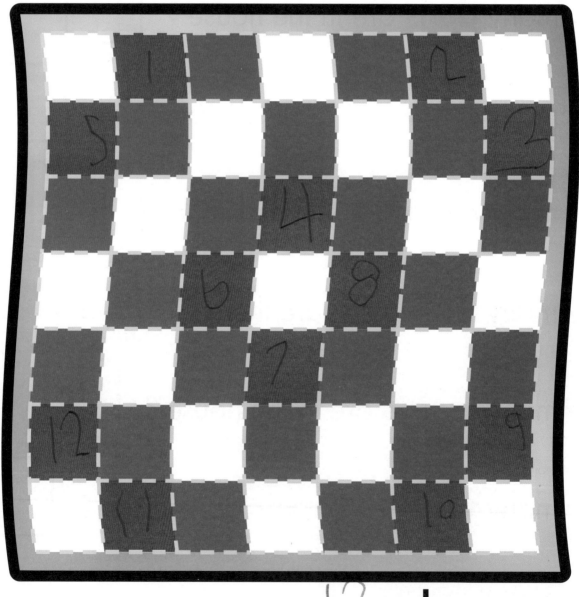

_12_ **red squares**

Guess the Missing Numbers

Look at the number sequence and write in each missing number.

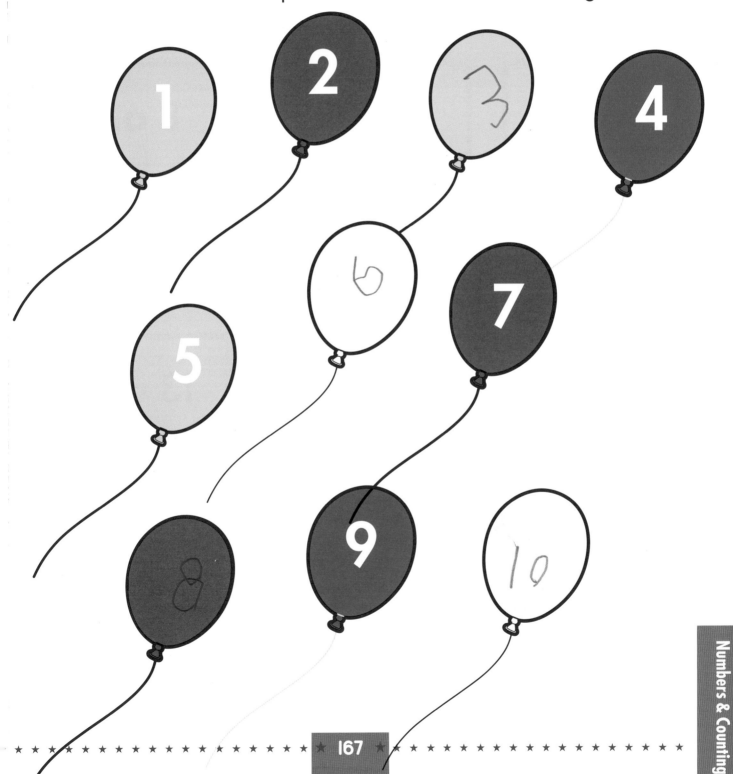

Which Is Greater?

Six is greater than five and ten is greater than nine. In the following exercise, circle the number in each box that is **GREATER**.

2 or (7)

(14) or 12

8 or (9)

3 or (12)

(19) or 18

5 or (15)

(9) or 6

13 or (18)

9 or (10)

4 or (17)

11 or (16)

(7) or 6

2 or (3)

Which Is Less?

Four is less than five and six is less than ten.
Circle the number in each box that is **LESS**.

10 or (8)	14 or (12)
8 or (6)	3 or (1)
20 or (10)	13 or (8)
19 or (11)	17 or (9)

Counting by Fives

Help the gorilla find the banana by counting by fives from 5 to 30.

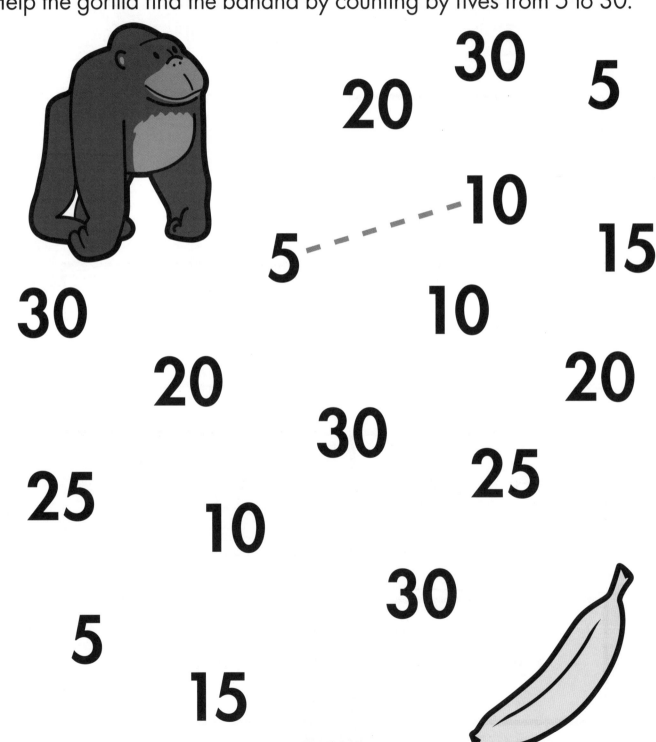

Complete the Pattern

In each row, write the number in the blank circles to complete the pattern.

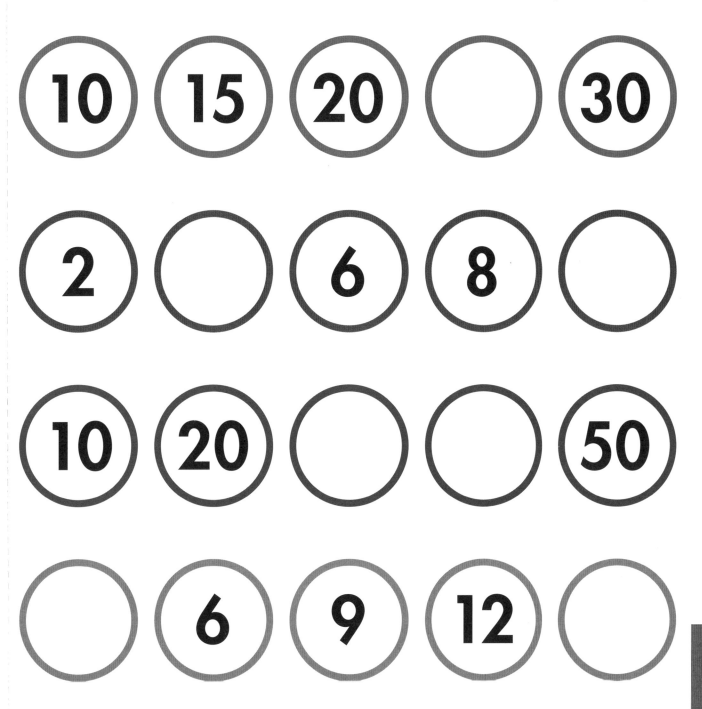

(10) (15) (20) ( ) (30)

(2) ( ) (6) (8) ( )

(10) (20) ( ) ( ) (50)

( ) (6) (9) (12) ( )

Counting 1–100

Here are all the numbers from **1** to **100**. How high can you count ?

1	2	3	4	5	6	7	8	9	10
11	12	13	14	15	16	17	18	19	20
21	22	23	24	25	26	27	28	29	30
31	32	33	34	35	36	37	38	39	40
41	42	43	44	45	46	47	48	49	50
51	52	53	54	55	56	57	58	59	60
61	62	63	64	65	66	67	68	69	70
71	72	73	74	75	76	77	78	79	80
81	82	83	84	85	86	87	88	89	90
91	92	93	94	95	96	97	98	99	100

Addition & Subtraction

ADDITION

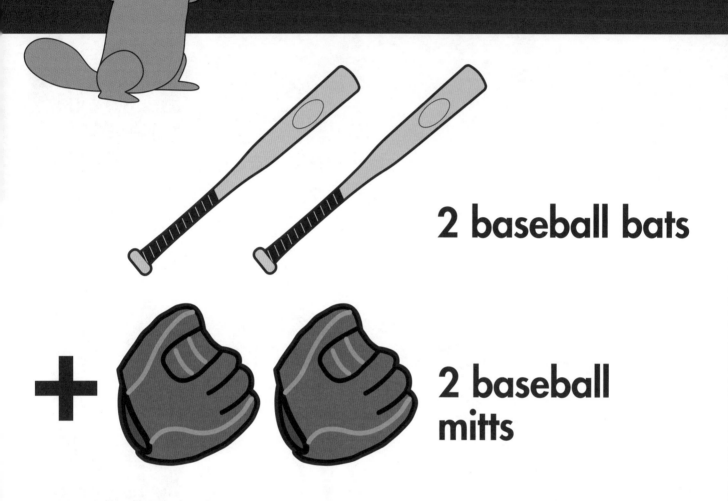

2 baseball bats

+ **2 baseball mitts**

4 bats and mitts

ADDITION

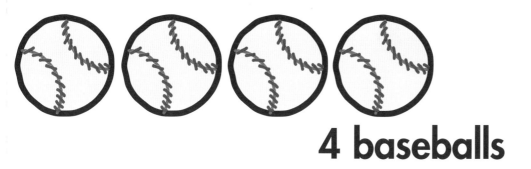

4 baseballs

+

2 baseballs

=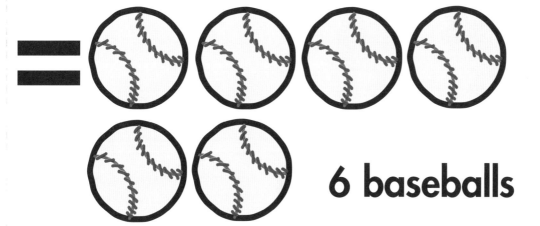

6 baseballs

ADDITION

3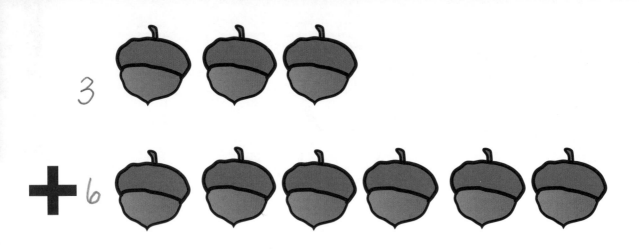

+ 6

___

= ___9 acorns

4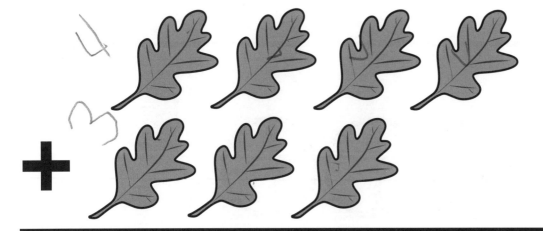

+ 3

___

= ___ leaves

ADDITION

+

= ____ **pumpkins**

+

= ____ **chipmunks**

ADDITION

4 apples + 2 apples = ___ apples

3 pears + 3 pears = ___ pears

ADDITION

ADDITION

+

= _____ boots

+

= _____ hats

ADDITION

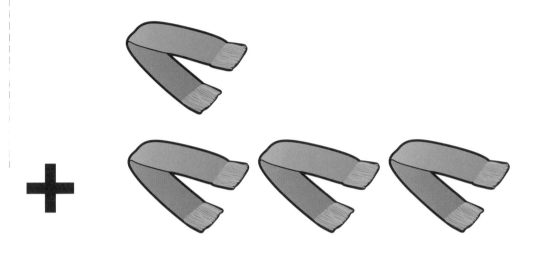

+

= _____ **scarves**

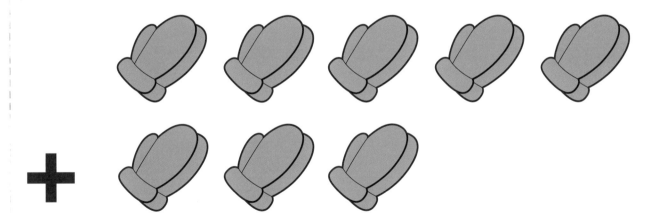

+

= _____ **mittens**

ADDITION

+

= _____ dolls

+

= _____ tops

ADDITION

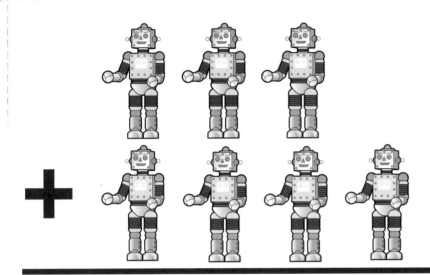

+

= _____ robots

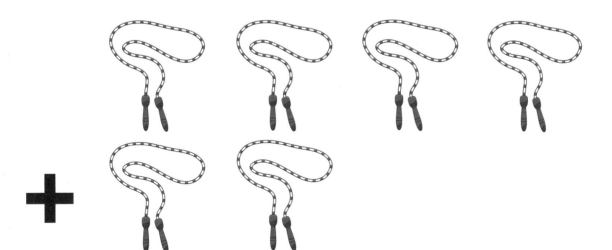

+

= _____ jump ropes

ADDITION

4 lizards +4 lizards= ___ lizards

2 snakes + 2 snakes = ___ snakes

ADDITION

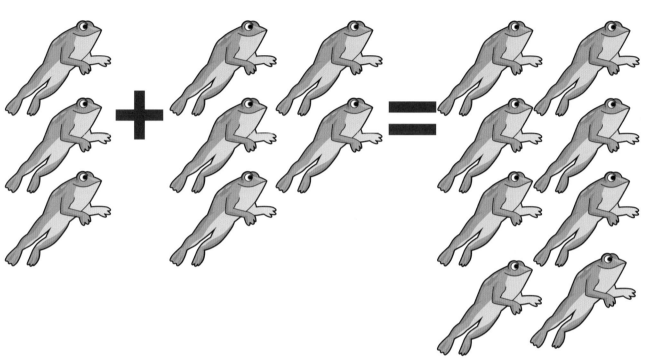

3 frogs + 5 frogs = ___ frogs

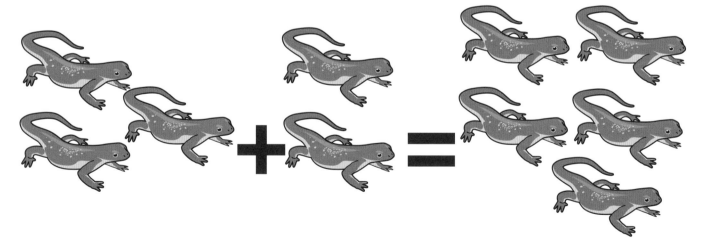

3 newts + 2 newts = ___ newts

ADDITION

+

= _____ scissors

+

= _____ erasers

ADDITION

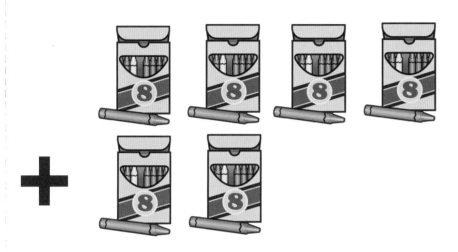

+

= _____ crayons

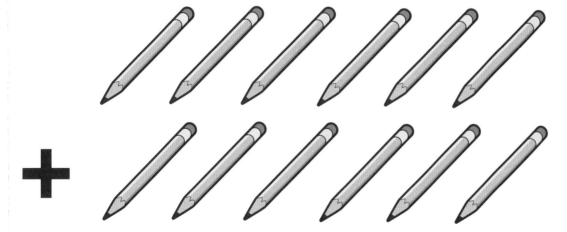

+

= _____ pencils

ADDITION

+

= ____ **peapods**

+

= ____ **tomatoes**

ADDITION

+

= ____ **carrots**

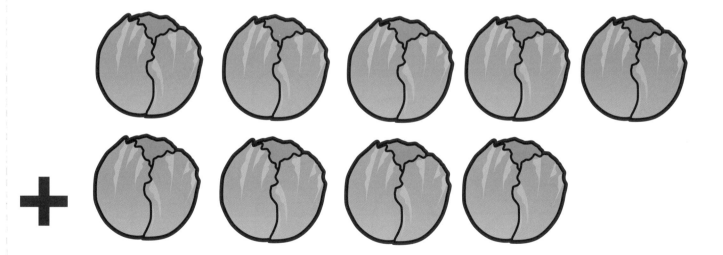

+

= ____ **lettuce**

189

ADDITION

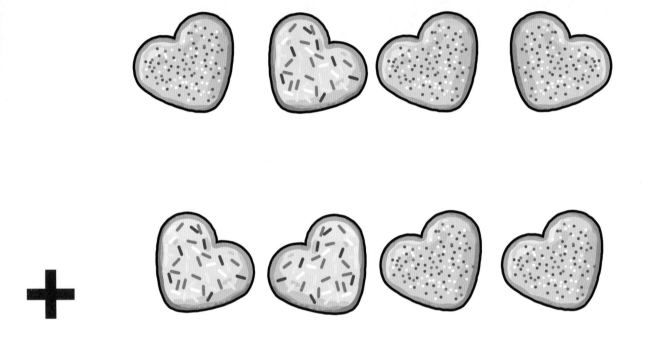

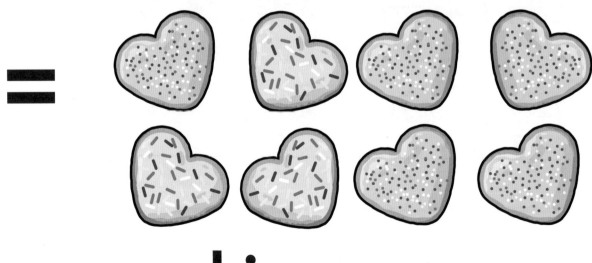

+

=

___ cookies

ADDITION

+

=

___ **cupcakes**

ADDITION

Practice your addition below.

$$5 + 0 = $$

$$3 + 2 = $$

$$1 + 4 = $$

$$2 + 2 = $$

$$3 + 3 = $$

$$5 + 2 = $$

$$1 + 2 = $$

$$6 + 1 = $$

$$8 + 2 = $$

$$4 + 5 = $$

$$2 + 1 = $$

$$7 + 2 = $$

SUBTRACTION

4 PB&J − 1 PB&J = ____ PB&J sandwiches

6 letters − 2 letters = ____ letters

SUBTRACTION

 mice

SUBTRACTION

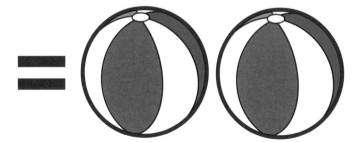

___ beach balls

SUBTRACTION

3 tricycles — 1 tricycle = ___ tricycles

7 acorns — 1 acorn = ___ acorns

SUBTRACTION

5 honey pots—2 honey pots= ___honeypots

4 ducklings — 2 ducklings = ___ ducklings

SUBTRACTION

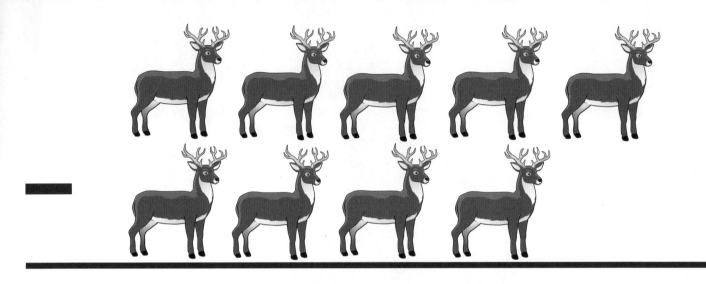

$-$

$=$ _____ deer

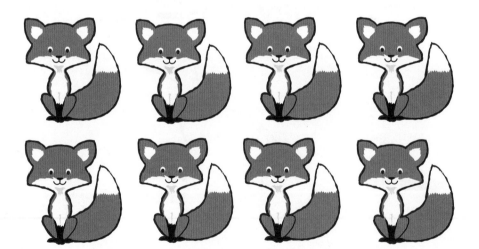

$-$

$=$ _____ foxes

SUBTRACTION

−

= _____ owls

−

= _____ bats

SUBTRACTION

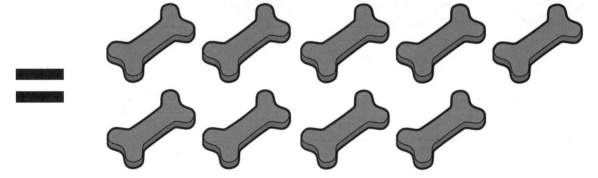

___ **dog bones**

SUBTRACTION

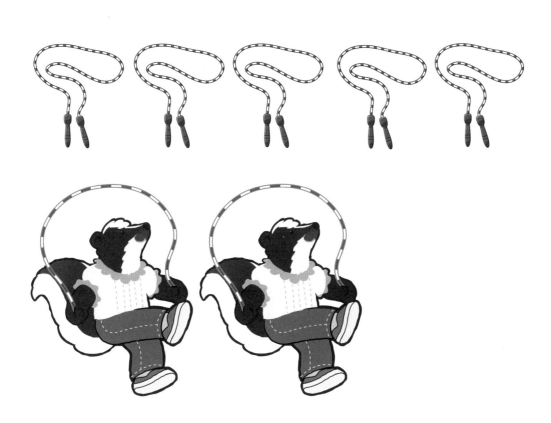

____ **jump ropes**

SUBTRACTION

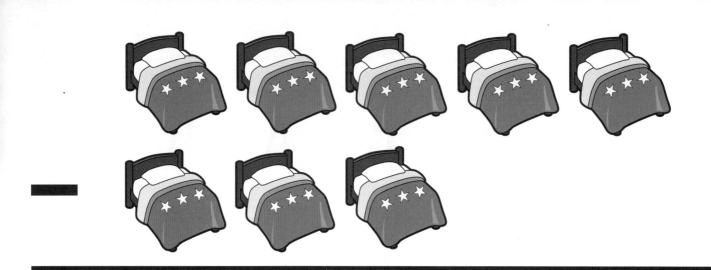

= _____ beds

= _____ bathtubs

SUBTRACTION

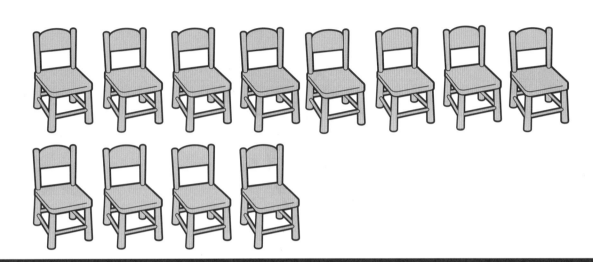

= _____ chairs

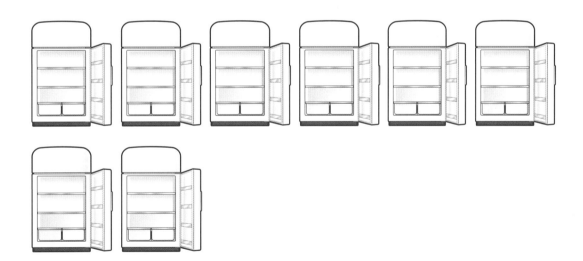

= _____ refrigerators

SUBTRACTION

10 tomatoes − 5 tomatoes = ___ tomatoes

8 shoes − 2 shoes = ___ shoes

SUBTRACTION

Practice your subtraction below.

$$\begin{array}{r} 2 \\ -\ 1 \\ \hline \end{array} \qquad \begin{array}{r} 3 \\ -\ 2 \\ \hline \end{array} \qquad \begin{array}{r} 4 \\ -\ 1 \\ \hline \end{array} \qquad \begin{array}{r} 5 \\ -\ 2 \\ \hline \end{array}$$

$$\begin{array}{r} 6 \\ -\ 3 \\ \hline \end{array} \qquad \begin{array}{r} 7 \\ -\ 6 \\ \hline \end{array} \qquad \begin{array}{r} 4 \\ -\ 2 \\ \hline \end{array} \qquad \begin{array}{r} 6 \\ -\ 5 \\ \hline \end{array}$$

$$\begin{array}{r} 8 \\ -\ 2 \\ \hline \end{array} \qquad \begin{array}{r} 2 \\ -\ 0 \\ \hline \end{array} \qquad \begin{array}{r} 9 \\ -\ 9 \\ \hline \end{array} \qquad \begin{array}{r} 5 \\ -\ 3 \\ \hline \end{array}$$

SUBTRACTION

−

= _____ fireman's hats

−

= _____ fire trucks

SUBTRACTION

−

= _____ firemen

−

= _____ fire hydrants

Subtraction

Practice your subtraction below.

100 A+

4 − 3 ――― 1	5 − 2 ――― 3	7 − 5 ――― 2	2 − 1 ――― 1
3 − 2 ――― 	6 − 4 ――― 2	9 − 8 ――― 1	6 − 5 ―――
1 − 1 ――― 0	7 − 2 ――― 5	8 − 3 ――― 5	4 − 2 ――― 2

Counting by 2

Fill in the blanks, counting by 2.

Counting by 10

Each tree has 10 apples. Add the apples by counting by 10s.

___ apples

Counting by 10

Help the boy get to the party by counting by 10s.

10 30 50 70 80

20 30 20 10 60

10 30 10 40 80 90 50

20 50 40 50 60 90 10

80 30 40 20 70 50 35

20 60 10 30

30 50 20 70

20 10 30 50

Next Number in Pattern

Write the next number in each pattern.

15 20 25 30 35 40 __

22 24 26 28 30 32 __

30 40 50 60 70 80 __

45 50 55 60 65 70 __

54 56 58 60 62 64 __

10 20 30 40 50 60 __

RED

ORANGE

YELLOW

Colors

GREEN

BLUE

PURPLE

Yellow & Purple

Color the objects below and fill in the names of the colors.

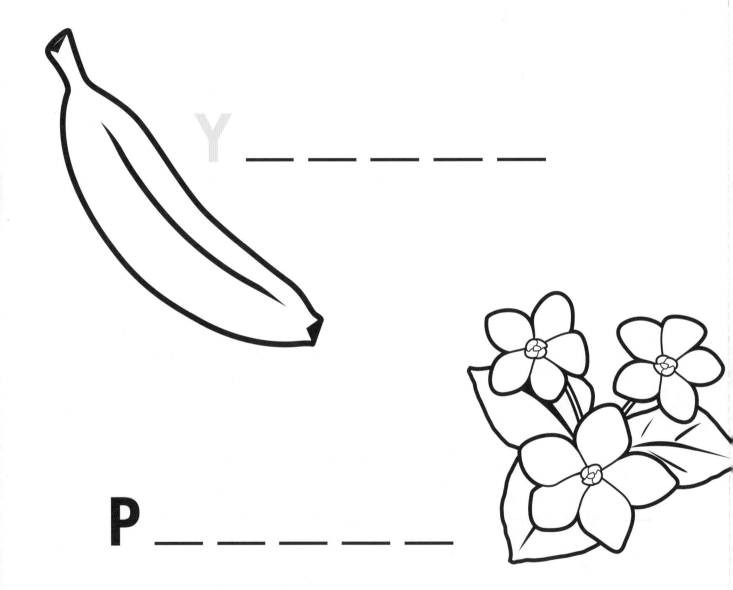

Y _ _ _ _ _ _

P _ _ _ _ _ _

Brown, Pink, & Orange

Color the objects below and fill in the names of the colors.

B _ _ _ _ _

P _ _ _ _

O _ _ _ _ _ _

Red, Blue, & Green

Color the objects below and fill in the names of the colors.

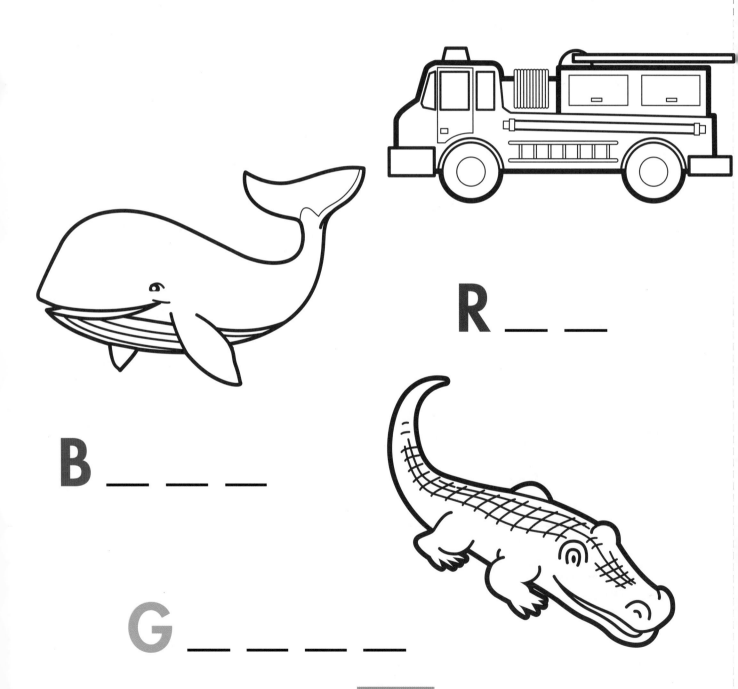

R _ _

B _ _ _

G _ _ _ _ _

Color by Numbers

Use the numbers fill in the picture below. What do you see?

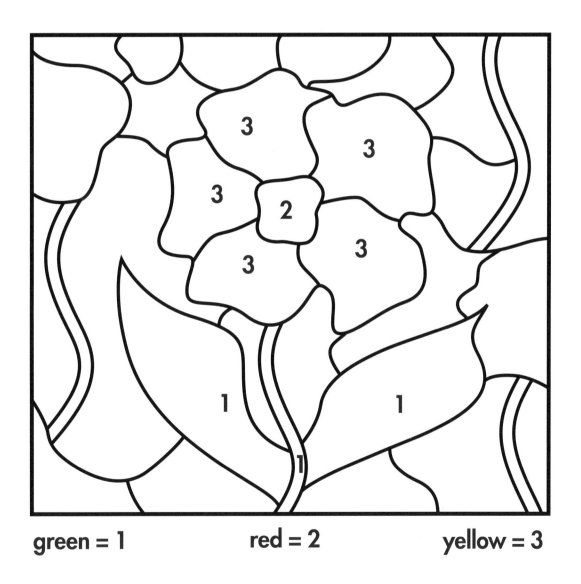

green = 1   **red = 2**   **yellow = 3**

Colors of the Rainbow

These are the colors in a rainbow.

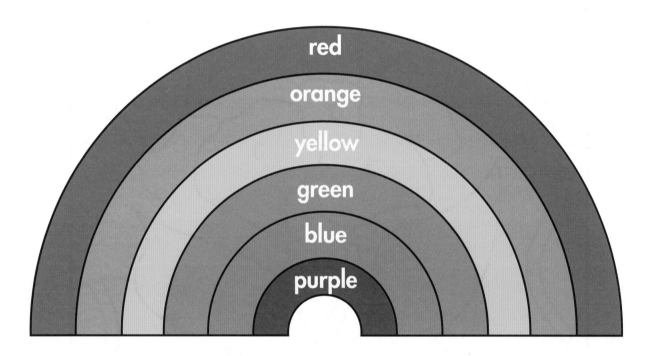

Match the Colors

Draw a line to match each color with its name.

red

green

blue

yellow

purple

Playing with Colors

Rocco the Raccoon is using his pallette to create new colors.
Look at what colors he mixes together to create green and brown.

Playing with Colors

Look at what two colors he mixes together to create orange, purple, pink, and gray.

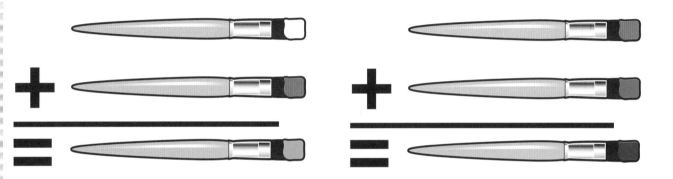

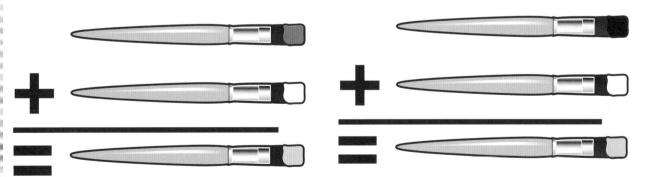

Playing with Colors

Can you fill in the missing colors?

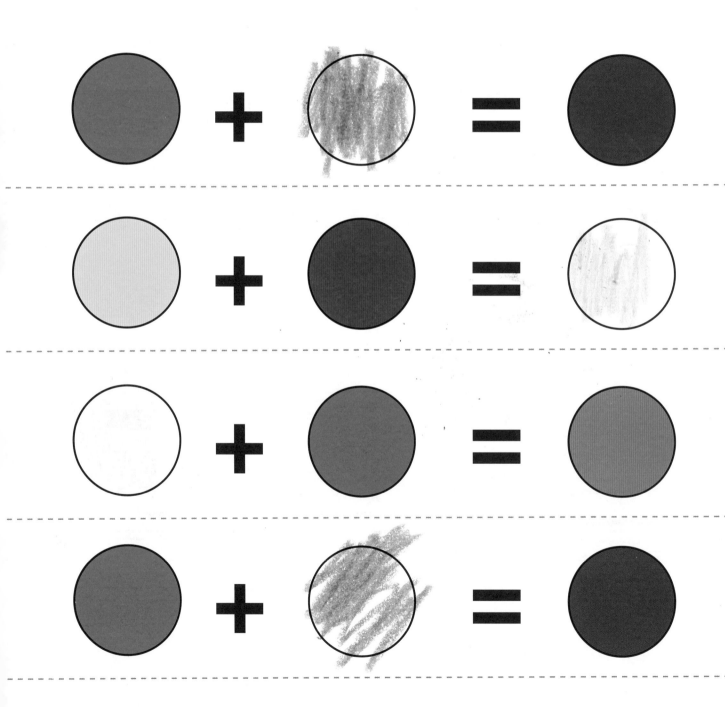

Playing with Colors

Fill in the missing colors from the rainbow

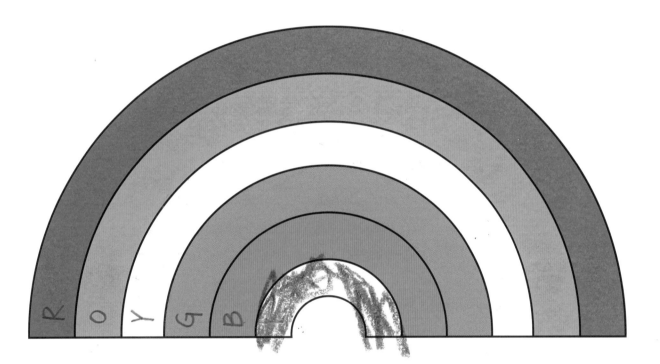

Playing with Colors

Fill in the palette to show all the colors of the rainbow.
Draw a line from the color to its name.

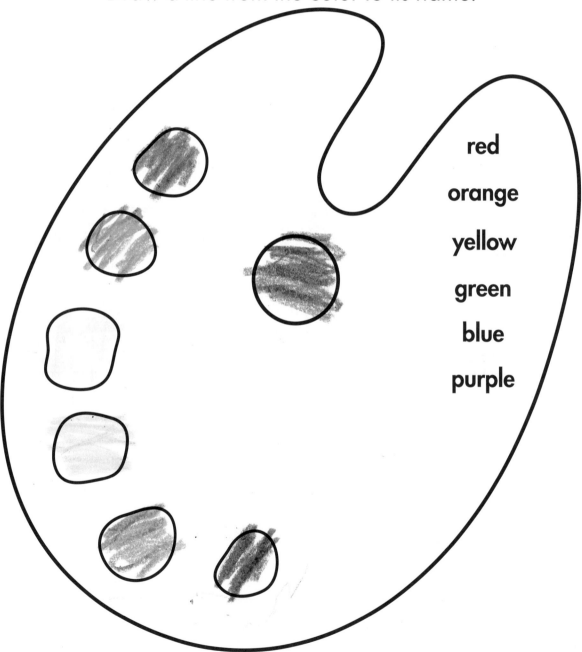

red

orange

yellow

green

blue

purple

SQUARE

CIRCLE

Shapes

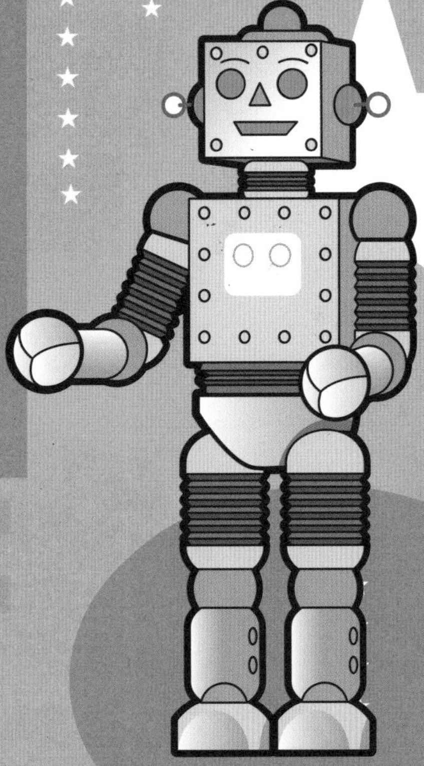

OVAL

RECTANGLE

DIAMOND

Shapes

Match the Shapes

Match each shape to its name. Then color in the shapes.

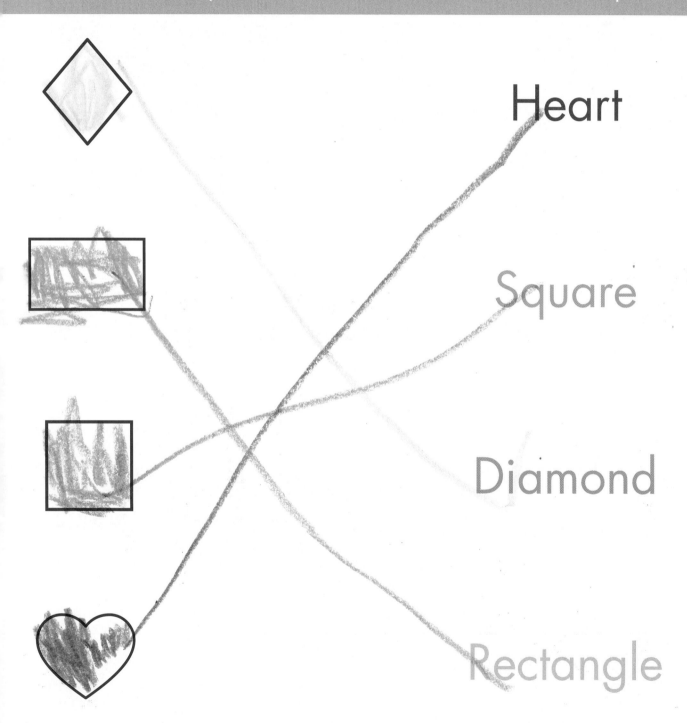

Heart

Square

Diamond

Rectangle

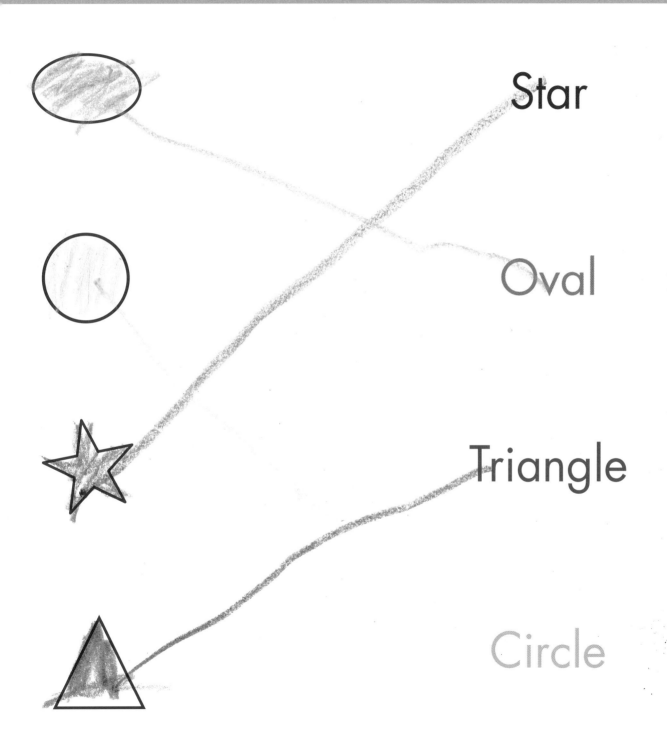

Star

Oval

Triangle

Circle

Draw the Shapes

Draw the shapes by following the dotted lines.

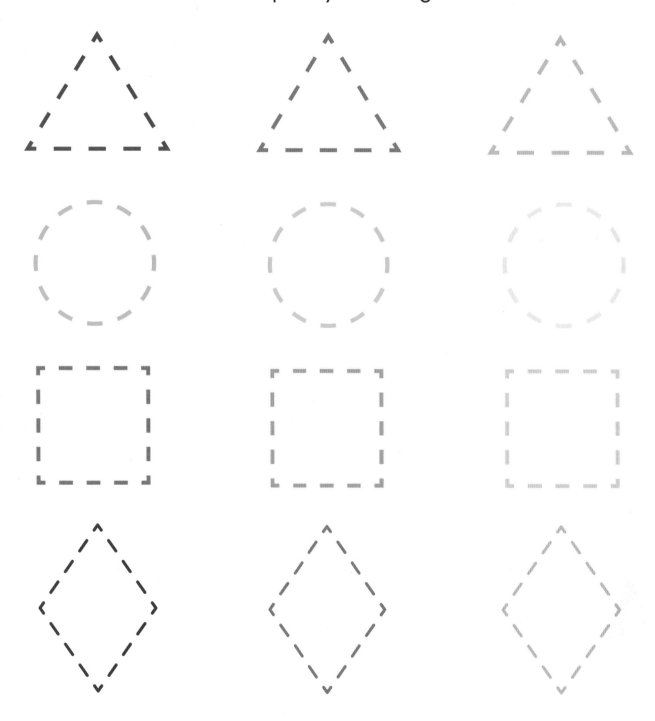

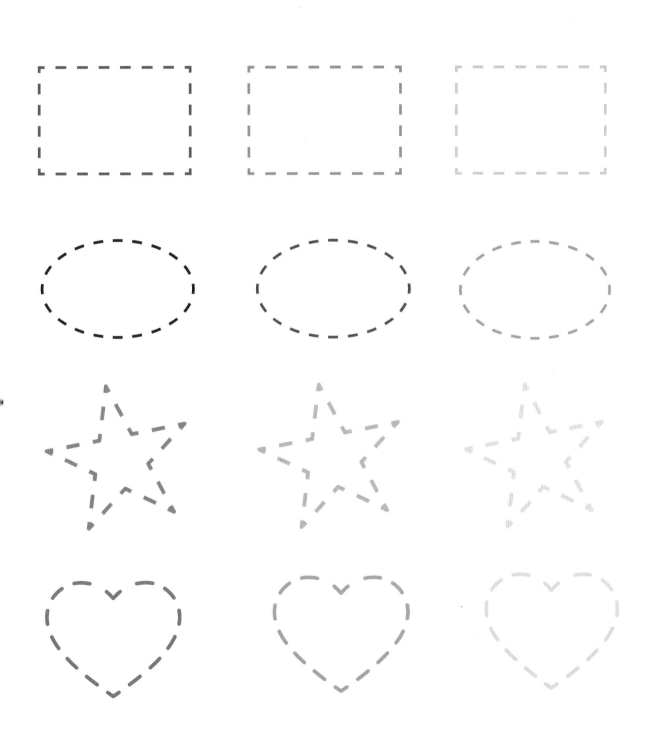

Find the Shapes

Connect the dotted line on the shapes in the town below and say the names aloud.

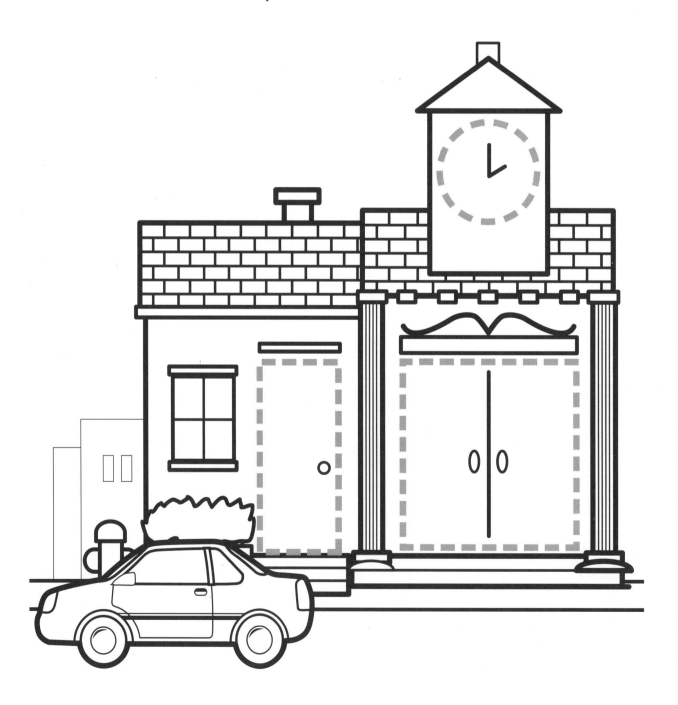

Can you find more squares, rectangles, triangles, ovals, and circles?
If so, color them in.

Complete the Shape

Trace the shapes to complete the pictures and color them in.

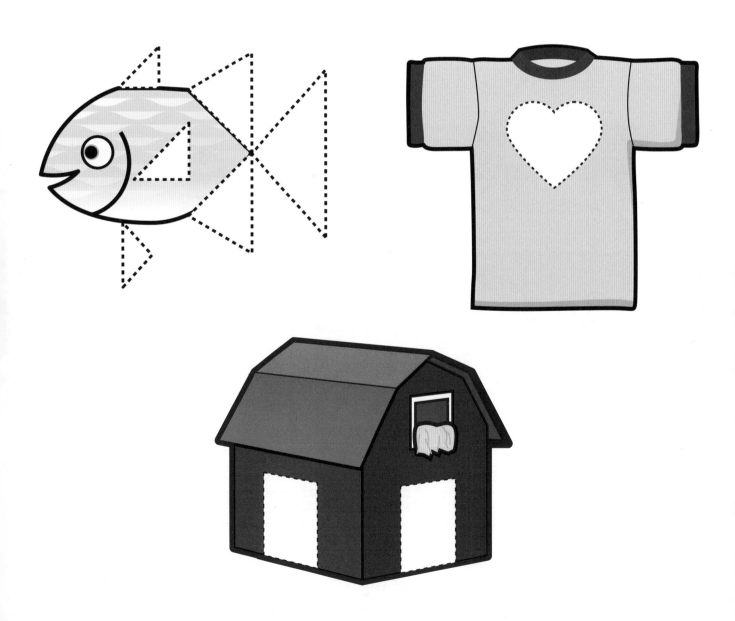

Color the Shapes

Find the shape in the pictures and color it the same
color as the shape at the bottom of the page.

Color the Shapes

Find the shape in the pictures and color it the same color as the shape at the bottom of the page.

Shapes

Color the Shapes

Find the shape in the pictures and color it the same color as the shape at the bottom of the page.

Find the Shapes

Can you find the triangle, square, oval, rectangle, circle, and star? If so, circle them.

Shapes

FIND THE CASTLE

Help the knight get to the castle. Draw a line along the path of triangles and circles to get there.

FUNNY FARM

Color in the shapes in the farm below.

Shapes

Complete the Pattern

Draw and color the shape that completes the pattern in each row.

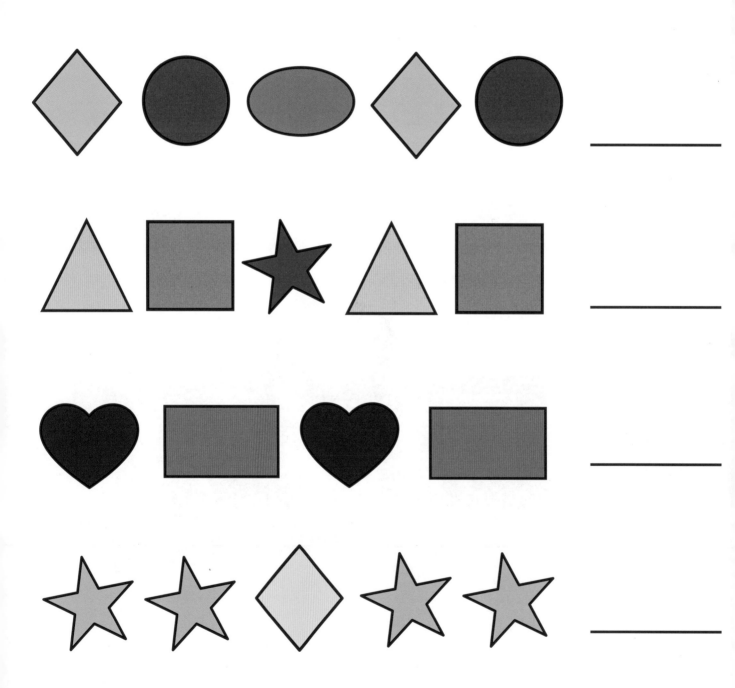

WEAK

Opposites

STRONG

OPPOSITES

Each picture below is the opposite of another.
Draw a line connecting each picture to its opposite.

fat

fast

slow

strong

weak

thin

happy

clean

hot

cold

sad

dirty

OPPOSITES

Some of the letters in this "opposites" crossword puzzle
have already been filled in to help you out.
Complete each answer by filling in the remaining letters.

ACROSS

4. OPPOSITE OF **HAPPY**

6. OPPOSITE OF **SHORT**

7. OPPOSITE OF **DAY**

DOWN

1. OPPOSITE OF **SLOW**

2. OPPOSITE OF **STRAIGHT**

3. OPPOSITE OF **THICK**

5. OPPOSITE OF **SMALL**

Our World

Wake Up!

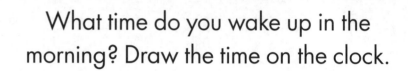

What time do you wake up in the morning? Draw the time on the clock.

What Happens Next?

Look at the pictures and write 1, 2, 3 and 4 below to put them in order.

___

___

___

___

Lunch

What time do you eat lunch? Draw the time on the clock.

Favorite Food

Draw a line from the picture to the word.

hamburger

pasta

pizza

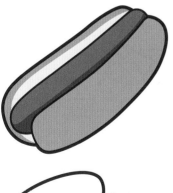

peanut butter & jelly

hot dog

Ready for Bed

Look at the pictures and write 1, 2, 3 and 4 below to put them in order.

Good Night

What time do you go to sleep? Draw the time on the clock.

24 Hours of My Day

Color one space on the graph for each hour you do something in your day. Remember, there are 24 hours in a day, so the colored spaces should add up to 24.

How many hours a day do you sleep?

How many hours a day do you play?

How many hours a day do you eat?

How many hours a day are you at school?

What Day is it Today?

What day is it today? Circle the word below.

Monday
Tuesday
Wednesday
Thursday
Friday
Saturday
Sunday

Day Scramble

Find the names of the days of the week and circle them.

```
G  Y  A  D  S  E  U  T
T  H  U  R  S  D  A  Y
S  U  N  D  A  Y  L  X
S  T  D  K  X  A  A  T
A  R  F  R  I  D  A  Y
T  A  Y  N  T  S  R  A
U  L  D  F  Q  E  I  D
R  E  E  L  R  N  C  N
D  A  F  L  Q  D  A  O
A  Y  A  D  S  E  U  M
Y  G  A  E  M  W  W  B
```

Calendar Month

Each month begins on day 1 and lasts either 29, 30, or 31 days. Fill in the dates missing from the calendar page below.

Sunday	Monday	Tuesday	Wednesday	Thursday	Friday	Saturday
						1
	3	4	5	6	7	8
9		11	12		14	15
16	17	18	19		21	
23	24		26	27		29
	31					

Birthdays

In what month is your birthday? Circle it in red.
Now circle the months of all the other birthdays in your family in blue.

January	May	September
February	June	October
March	July	November
April	August	December

My Family

Everyone's family is different. What do you call your parents? Write it on the lines below.

_____
mother

_____
father

What are the names of your brothers and sisters?.
Write them on the lines below.

sister   **brother**   **baby**

_____

_____

What do you call your grandmothers and grandfathers? Write ithem on the lines below.

grandfather

_____

_____

_____

What are the names of your aunts, uncles, and cousins?. Write them on the lines below.

uncle

aunt

cousins

_____

_____

My House

There are many rooms in a house. Draw a line between the names and the rooms.

bathroom   bedroom   kitchen   living room

Draw a picture of the view outside your bedroom window.

People in My Neighborhood

Match the people in your neighborhood to the correct picture by writing it on the blank lines.

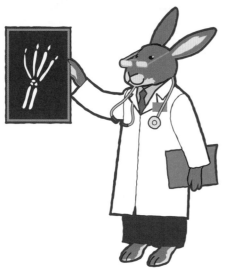

_ _ _ _ _ _ _ _ _

_ _ _ _ _ _ _ _ _

fireman
chef
dentist
builder
policeman
teacher
doctor

_ _ _ _ _ _ _ _ _ _ _ _ _

_ _ _ _ _ _ _ _ _ _

_ _ _ _ _ _ _ _ _

Our World

Pets

Animals that live with people are pets.
Circle the animals that are pets.

Mammals

Mammals are warm-blooded, have fur or hair, and usually do not lay eggs. Here are some mammals to color.

Birds

Birds are warm-blooded, have feathers and wings, and lay eggs.
Circle the birds below.

Reptiles

Reptiles are cold-blooded, have scales or bony plates, and some lay eggs. Draw a line from the reptile to its name.

lizard

turtle

alligator

snake

Insects

Insects have six legs and a body with three parts called the head, the thorax, and the abdomen. Circle the insects in the garden.

The 5 Senses:
HEARING

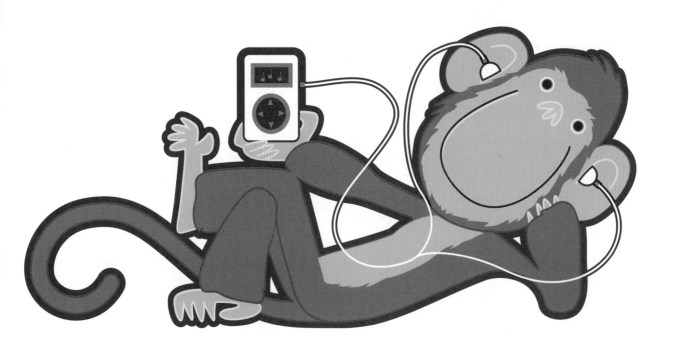

List four songs that you know all of the words.

_____   _____

_____   _____

Color in all of the musical instruments.

The 5 Senses: SIGHT

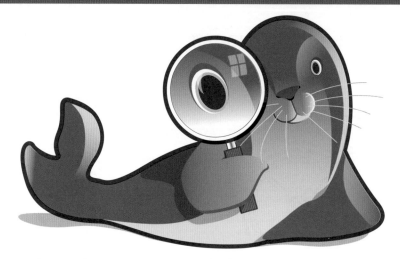

Look in the mirror and draw what you see.

Can you see the four differences between these two images?
If so, circle them.

The 5 Senses: SMELL

Find the following words on the next page for things that smell good.

flowers
cookies
perfume
bread
oranges
campfire

List your favorite smells.

_____   _____

_____   _____

P	Y	A	D	S	B	U	B
E	H	U	R	S	R	A	R
R	U	S	D	A	E	L	E
F	T	R	K	X	A	A	E
U	S	E	R	I	D	A	R
M	E	W	N	T	S	R	I
E	G	O	F	Q	E	I	F
R	N	L	L	R	N	C	P
D	A	F	L	Q	D	A	M
A	R	A	D	S	E	U	A
C	O	O	K	I	E	S	C

The Five Senses: Taste

What are your four favorite foods? Write them below.

_____   _____

_____   _____

Circle the food below that tastes sweet.

The Five Senses: Touch

What hurts when you touch it? Write a list below.

_____   _____

_____   _____

Which animals are soft to the touch?
Circle them below.

The Seasons: Winter

Below is a farm in the winter. Color the image below.

Winter is the coldest season. Circle the months of winter.

January **February** **March** **April** **May** **June** **July**

August **September** **October** **November** **December**

Circle the clothes that you wear in the winter.

The Seasons: Spring

Below is a farm in spring. Color the image below.

Spring occurs between winter and summer. Circle the months of spring.

January **February** **March** **April** **May** **June** **July**

August **September** **October** **November** **December**

"April showers bring May flowers" Look at the pictures and write 1, 2, 3 and 4 below to put them in order.

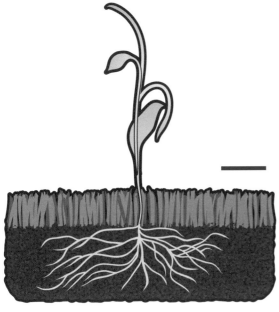

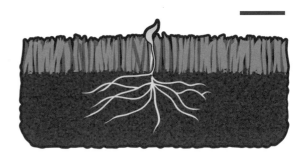

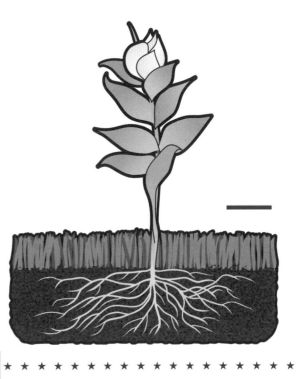

The Seasons: Summer

Below is a farm in summer. Color the image below.

Summer is the hottest season. Circle the months of summer.

January **February** **March** April May June **July**

August September **October** **November** **December**

A Day at the Beach

Help Hannah find her beach ball. Draw a line along the path that shows things you bring to the beach.

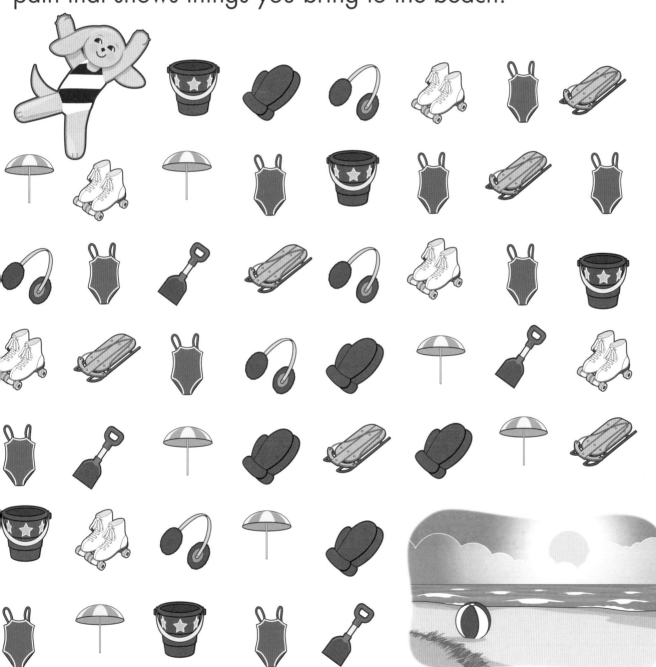

The Seasons: Fall

Below is a farm in fall. Color the image below.

Fall occurs between summer and winter. Circle the months of fall.

January **February** **March** **April** **May** **June** **July**

August **September** **October** **November** **December**

True or False ?

During the **spring** the leaves on the trees turn green.
TRUE or FALSE

During the **summer** I wear my snowsuit to keep warm.
TRUE or FALSE

When it is **fall** the leaves turn brown and fall to the ground.
TRUE or FALSE

During the **winter** I sometimes play in the snow.
TRUE or FALSE

During the **spring** I celebrate Halloween.
TRUE or FALSE

During the **summer** I don't have to go to school.
TRUE or FALSE

During the **fall** I begin school.
TRUE or FALSE

During the **winter** it's so hot that I spend most of my time outside.
TRUE or FALSE

Telling Time

Clocks and watches have a big hand to tell the minutes and a little hand to tell the hour. Look at the picture below. The hour hand is pointing to the 1 and the minute hand is pointing to the 12 (or 0 minutes). It is 1:00, or one o'clock.

In this picture, the hour hand is between numbers 1 and 2, and the minute hand is pointing to the number 30, so it is 1:30, or one thirty.

Telling Time

Each of the four clocks is telling you a different time.
Write down what time it is under each clock.

__ __ : __ __ __ __

__ __ : __ __ __ __

__ __ : __ __ __ __

__ __ : __ __ __ __

What Time Is it?

Fill in the correct time on each clock.

This is the time I have my breakfast.

This is the time I go to school.

This is the time I have my lunch.

This is the time I have my dinne

This is the time I take a bath.

This is the time I go to bed.

What Time Is it?

Complete the pattern for each set of clocks by drawing
a big hand and a little hand on the clocks that are blank.

What Time Is it?

Complete the pattern for each set of clocks by drawing a big hand and a little hand on the clocks that are blank.

Match the Time

Draw a line between the two clocks with the same time.

Weather

What is the weather like in your neighborhood today?
Choose some of the words below to describe what it is like outside.

Rainy **Warm** **Sunny** **Cloudy** **Hot**
Windy **Snowing** **Cold**

_____   _____

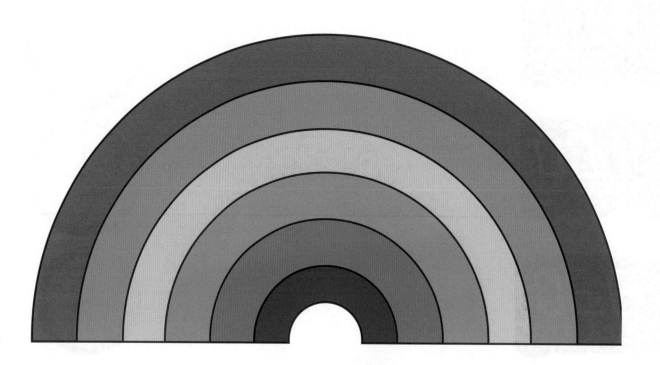

Water can be in three states, either a solid, a liquid, or a gas.
Draw a line between the picture and its state.

Solid

Liquid

Gas

Road Safety

When you are riding a bike or scooter on the street, always wear a helmet. Also, ride in the same direction as the cars.

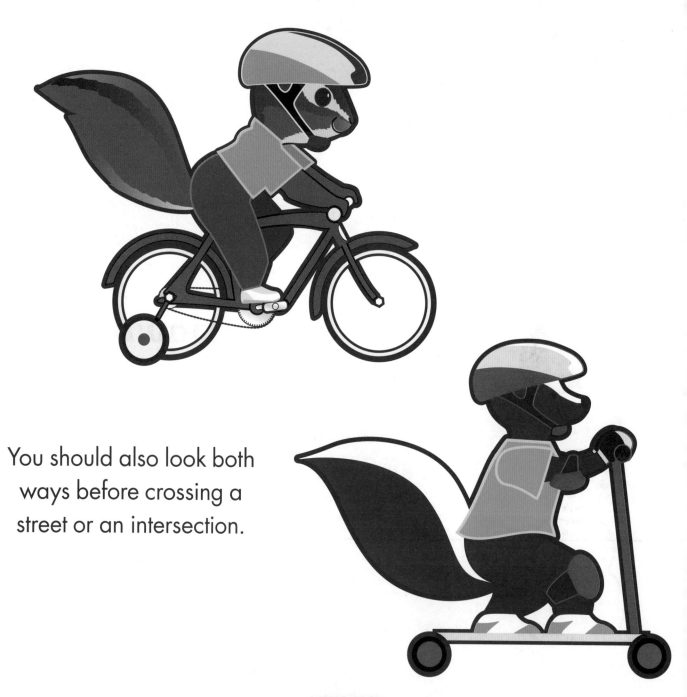

You should also look both ways before crossing a street or an intersection.

When you are riding on the street, you must also obey street signs.
Fill in the letters to complete the sign.

S _ _ _ _

Y _ _ _ _

C _ _ _ _ _ _ _ _ _

O _ _ _   _ _ _

Our World

Counting Money

1 penny is 1 cent or 1¢

1 nickel is 5 cents or 5¢
5 pennies = 1 nickel or 5¢

1 dime is 10 cents or 10¢
10 pennies = 1 dime or 10¢

2 nickels = 1 dime or 10¢

1 quarter is 25 cents or 25¢

Counting Money

Each set of coins below is worth 25 cents.

 =

One quarter = 5 nickels

 =

One quarter = 3 nickels and 1 dime

 =

One quarter = 1 nickel and 2 dimes

 =  +

Our World

Counting Money

Count the money in each row and write the answer on the line.

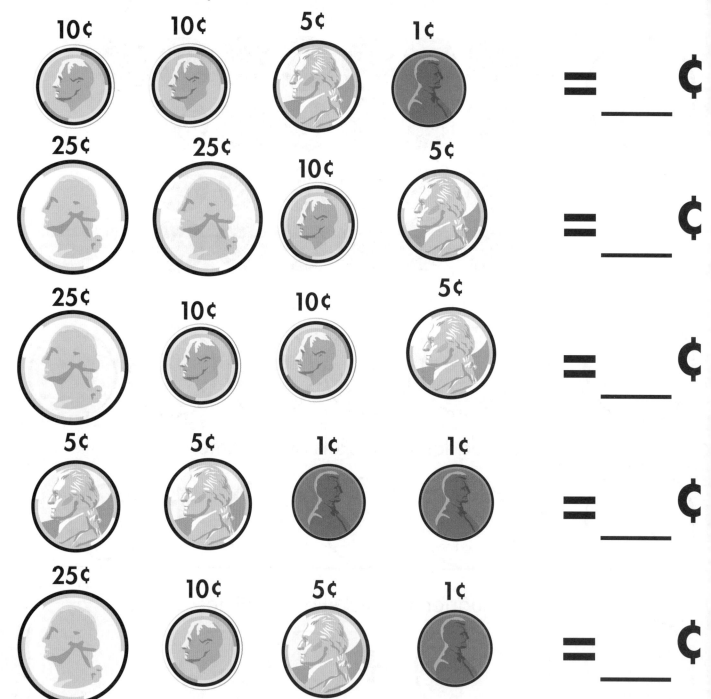

10¢   10¢   5¢   1¢   = ___ ¢

25¢   25¢   10¢   5¢   = ___ ¢

25¢   10¢   10¢   5¢   = ___ ¢

5¢   5¢   1¢   1¢   = ___ ¢

25¢   10¢   5¢   1¢   = ___ ¢

Counting Money

If you had these coins in your piggy bank,
how much money would you have?

How Much Does It Cost?

Add up the amount of money in each set of coins and then draw a line to the present that has that number on its price tag.

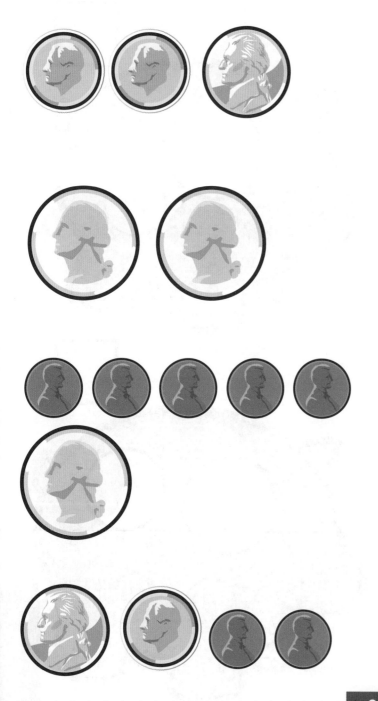

How Much Does It Cost?

Add up the amount of money in each set of coins and then draw a line to the present that has that number on its price tag.

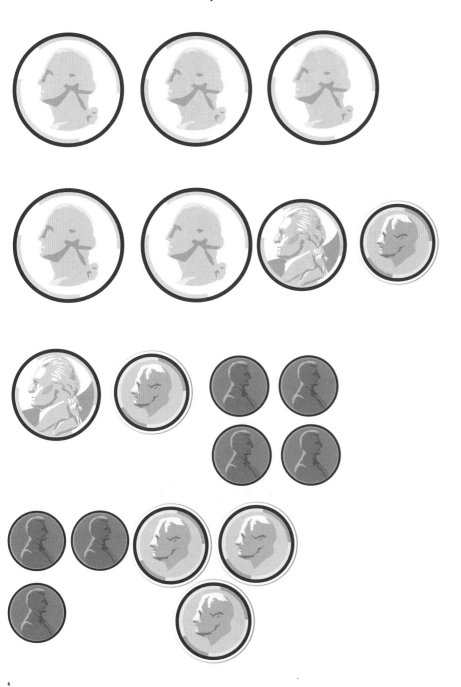 

The Continents

NORTH
AMERICA

SOUTH
AMERICA

ANTARCTICA

The world is divided into seven land masses known as continents. The map below shows the names of the continents. Circle the continent where you live.

ASIA

EUROPE

AFRICA

AUSTRALIA

Word Search

Find and circle the names of the continents listed below
They might be across or up-and-down.

ASIA   **AFRICA**

EUROPE   **AUSTRALIA**

```
G  A  S  I  A  B  L  E
E  U  R  O  P  E  M  S
F  S  G  B  R  T  L  X
D  T  H  K  X  M  A  M
Y  R  C  L  J  P  F  W
B  A  U  L  T  D  R  H
G  L  T  F  Q  Z  I  A
U  I  E  L  R  B  C  P
W  A  F  L  Q  D  A  N
```

Country

Below is the continent of North America. Which country is the United States of America? Circle it.

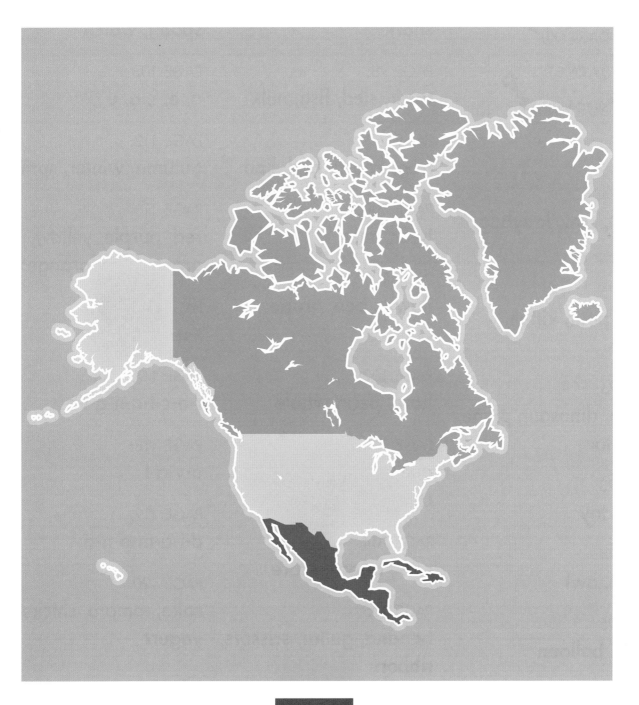

Answers

PAGE 66:

PAGE 74:
rabbit, cow, ladybug, table

PAGE 75:
boat, pear, kitten, skates

PAGE 76:
clown, dinosaur, plane, alligator

PAGE 93:
toilet, toy

PAGE 94:
house, owl

PAGE 95:
book, balloon

PAGE 96:
fawn, autumn

PAGE 97:
turtle, bird, farmer, shark

PAGE 98:
truck, sled, fish, milk

PAGE 99:
frog, zebra, bed, lion

PAGE 100:
bear, deer

PAGE 101:
flower, bee, grapes, quilt

PAGE 102:
hare, pear, whale

PAGE 103:
queen, peanut, apple, chicken

PAGE 104:
corn, board, score

PAGE 105:
banana, guitar, scissors, ribbon

PAGE 106:
map, eraser, gate, slide

PAGE 107:
zipper, ice cream, fairy, spoon, watch

PAGE 108:
a, e, i, o, u

PAGE 112:
autumn, winter, spring

PAGE 113:
red, purple, yellow, green, blue, orange

PAGE 116:
s-q-u-a-r-e

PAGE 117:
r-e-c-t-a-n-g-l-e

PAGE 118:
o-v-a-l

PAGE 119:
d-i-a-m-o-n-d

PAGE 120:
cake, tomato, chicken, yogurt

PAGE 121:

monkey, kangeroo, giraffe, tiger

PAGE 122:

spider, drum, penguin, clover

PAGE 123:

shirt, goat, rhino, lamp

PAGE 124:

gorilla, apple, alligator

PAGE 125:

squirrel, parrot

PAGE 126:

nest, pasta, stroller, puppy

PAGE 127:

bike, mittens, violin, mouse

PAGE 128:

catch, crash, dish, trash, match

PAGE 129:

white, thunder, wheel, three, thumb, whisper, whale, think

PAGE 130:

PAGE 133:

3 buckets, 2 castles, 3 balls

PAGE 158:

10 bubbles

PAGE 159:

9 items

PAGE 160:

9 inches, 15 inches

PAGE 161:

8 inches, 10 inches, 5 inches

PAGE 162:

13 red, 6 no spots, 8 yellow, 6 green

PAGE 165:

2 dolls, 4 drawers, 2 chairs, 5 windows, 2 lamps, 2 windowboxes

PAGE 166:

12 red squares

PAGE 167:

3, 6, 8, 10

PAGE 168:

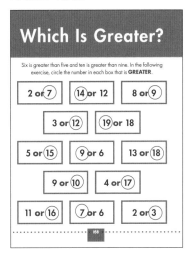

PAGE 169:

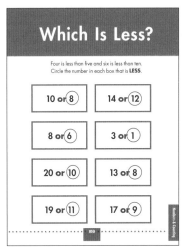

PAGE 170:

PAGE 171:

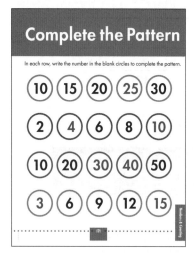

PAGE 176:
9 acorns, 7 leaves

PAGE 177:
5 pumpkins, 5 chipmunks

PAGE 178:
6 apples, 6 pears

PAGE 179:
4 cherries, 5 grapes, 5 strawberries

PAGE 180:
9 boots, 6 hats

PAGE 181:
4 scarves, 8 mittens

PAGE 182:
10 dolls, 7 tops

PAGE 183:
7 robots, 6 jump ropes

PAGE 184:
8 lizards, 4 snakes

PAGE 185:
8 frogs, 5 newts

PAGE 186:
10 scissors, 9 erasers

PAGE 187:
6 crayons, 12 pencils

PAGE 188:
9 peapods, 7 tomatoes

PAGE 189:
12 carrots, 9 lettuce

PAGE 190:
8 cookies

PAGE 191:
8 cupcakes

PAGE 192:

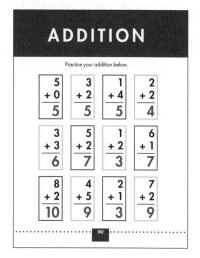

PAGE 193:
3 sandwiches, 4 letters

PAGE 194:
2 mice

PAGE 195:
2 beach balls

PAGE 196:
2 tricycles, 6 acorns

PAGE 197:
3 honey pots, 2 ducklings

PAGE 198:
1 deer, 0 foxes

PAGE 199:
5 owls, 2 bats

PAGE 200:
9 dog bones

PAGE 201:

3 jump ropes

PAGE 202:

2 beds, 3 bathtubs

PAGE 203:

4 chairs, 4 refrigerators

PAGE 204:

5 tomatoes, 6 shoes

PAGE 205:

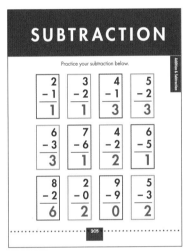

PAGE 206:

1 fireman's hat, 2 fire trucks

PAGE 207:

2 firemen, 3 fire hydrants

PAGE 208:

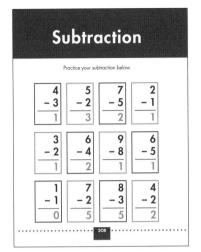

PAGE 209:

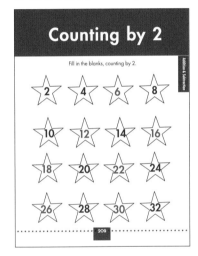

PAGE 210:

50 apples

PAGE 211:

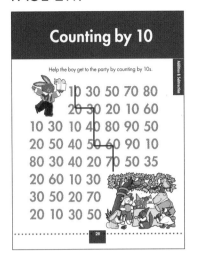

PAGE 212:

PAGE 214:

yellow, purple

PAGE 215:

brown, pink, orange

PAGE 216:

red, blue, green

PAGE 219:

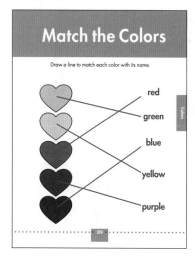

PAGE 222:

blue, green, yellow, blue

PAGE 226:

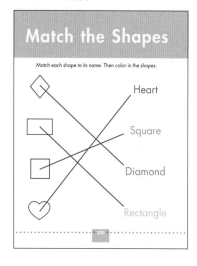

PAGE 227:

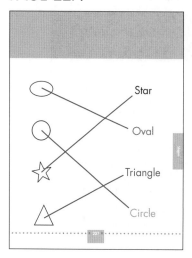

PAGE 237:

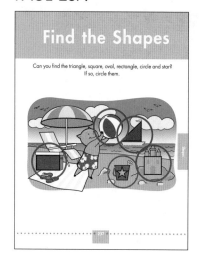

PAGE 238:

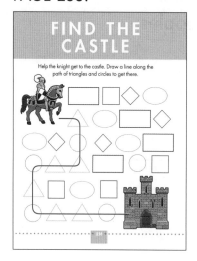

PAGE 240:

green oval, blue star, purple heart, yellow diamond

PAGE 242:

PAGE 243:

PAGE 244:

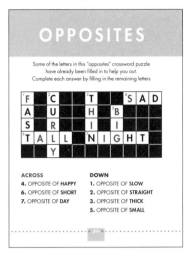

PAGE 250:

PAGE 262:

doctor, teacher, chef, fireman

PAGE 263:

policeman, builder, dentist

PAGE 264:

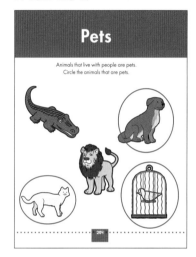

PAGE 247:

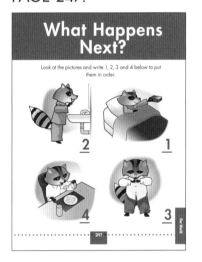

PAGE 255:

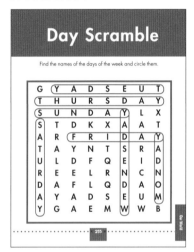

PAGE 265:

PAGE 249:

PAGE 260:

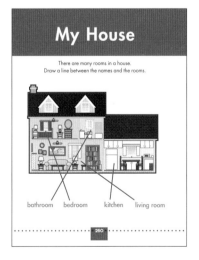

PAGE 267:

PAGE 273:

PAGE 279:

PAGE 268:

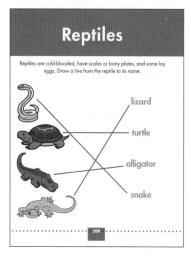

PAGE 275:

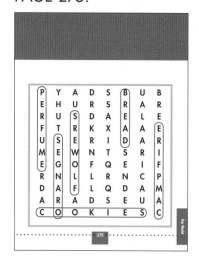

PAGE 280:

December, January, February, March

PAGE 281:

PAGE 269:

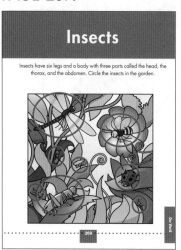

PAGE 277:

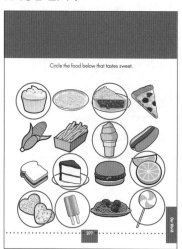

PAGE 282:

March, April, May, June

PAGE 283:

PAGE 284:

June, July, August,
September

PAGE 285:

PAGE 286:

September, October,
November, December

PAGE 287:

true, false, true, true,
false, true, true, false

PAGE 289:

4:00, 8:30, 11:30, 9:00

PAGE 291:

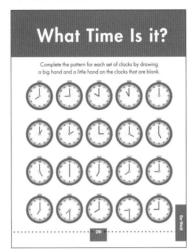

PAGE 292:

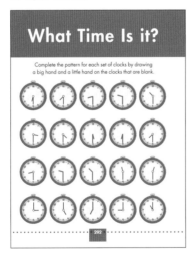

PAGE 293:

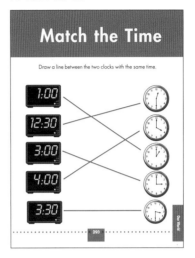

PAGE 295:

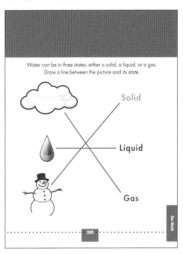

PAGE 297:

stop, yield, crosswalk,
one way

PAGE 300:

26 cents, 65 cents, 50
cents, 12 cents, 41 cents

PAGE 301:

5 cents, 36 cents, 17
cents, 32 cents

PAGE 303:

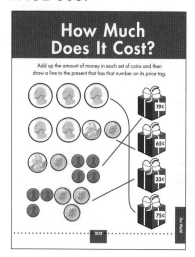

PAGE 306:

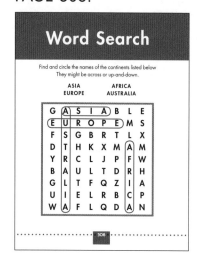

Suggested Reading List

The following is a list of books appropriate for your pre-first grade child. We recommend setting aside some time each day to read with your child. The more your child reads, the faster he or she will acquire other skills.

Abe Lincoln and the Muddy Pig by Stephen Krensky

Adelita by Tomie DePaola

The Adventures of Taxi Dog by Debra Barracca

Albert by Donna Jo Napoli

Alexander and the Terrible, Horrible, No Good, Very Bad Day by Judith Viorst

Amanda Pig and Her Best Friend Lollipop by Jean Van Leeuwen

Amazing Snakes by Alexandra Parsons

Amelia Bedelia by Peggy Parish

Anasi and the Magic Stick by Eric Kimmel

Arthur and the Best Coach Ever by Stephen Krensky

Arthur's Teacher Moves In by Marc Brown

Bedtime for Frances by Russell Hoban

Brown Bear, Brown Bear, What Do You See? by Bill Martin

The Caboose Who Got Loose by Bill Peet

Cam Jansen and the Birthday Mystery by David Adler

Caps for Sale by Esphyr Slobodkina

The Case of the Spooky Sleepover, Kigsaw Jones Mystery #44 by James Preller

Caves by Larry Dane Brimner

Chester's Way by Kevin Henkes

Chicken Soup with Rice, A Book of Months by Maurice Sendak

Daisy Comes Home by Jan Brett

Danny and the Dinosaur Go to Camp by Syd Hoff

Do You Want to Be My Friend? by Eric Carl

The Dog that Pitched a No-Hitter by Christopher Matt

Dogs Don't Wear Sneakers by Laura Numeroff

Fannie in the Kitchen by Deborah Hopkinson

Flat Stanley by Jeff Brown

Fox on the Job by James Marshall

Franklin Rides a Bike by Paulette Bourgeois

Freckle Juice by Judy Blume

Frog and Toad Are Friends by Arnold Lobel

The Friendship Tree by Kathy Caple

Giant Children: Poems by Brod Bagert

Ginger Jumps by Lisa Ernst

The Giving Tree by Shel Silverstein

Gloria's Way by Ann Cameron

Good Night Dinosaurs by Judy Sierra

Good Night, Good Knight by Shelley Moore Thomas

Grandpa's Teeth by Rod Clement

The Great Kapok Tree: A Tale of the Amazon Rain Forest by Lynne Cherry

Henry Mudge and the Tall Tree House by Cynthia Rylant

The Honest-to-Goodness Truth by Patricia McKissack

If You Give a Mouse a Cookie by Laura Numeroff

If You Give a Pig a Pancake by Laura Numeroff

If You Hopped Like a Frog by David Schwartz

Inspector Hopper by Doug Cushman

Iris and Walter: The Sleepover by Elissa Haden Guest

Is Your Mama a Llama? by Deborah Guarino

Jelly Beans for Sale by Bruce McMillan

Junie B. Jones Smells Something Fishy by Barbara Park

Kate and the Beanstalk by Mary Pope Osborne

Leola and the Honeybears by Melodye Benson Rosales

Lilly's Purple Plastic Purse by Kevin Henkes

The Listening Walk by Paul Showers

The Little Engine That Could by Watty Piper

Make Way for Ducklings by Robert McCloskey

Martha Blah Blah by Susan Meddaugh

Martin's Big Words: the Life of Dr. Martin Luther King Jr. by Doreen Rappaport

Max and Jax in Second Grade by Jerdie Nolen

Monkey Business by Esphyr Slobodkina

Moving Molly by Shirley Hughes

Mrs. Katz and Tush by Patricia Polacco

Newt by Matt Novak

Nibble, Nibble, Jenny Archer by Ellen Conford

Olivia by Ian Falconer

One Dark Night by Lisa Wheeler

Pigs at Odds by Amy Axelrod

Pinky and Rex and the Just-Right Pet by James Howe

Platypus and the Lucky Day by Chris Riddell

Play Ball, Amelia Bedelia by Audrey Wood

Robots Don't Catch Chicken Pox by Debbie Dadey and Marcia Thornton Jones

Shoeless Joe and Black Betsy by Phil Bilder

A Sip of Aesop by Jane Yolen

Stella Louella's Runaway Book by Lisa Ernst

Stellaluna by Janell Cannon

Take Me Out of the Bathtub by Alan Katz

Ten Apples Up on Top! by Mercer Mayer

Three Stories You Can Read to Your Dog by Sara Swan Miller

Together by Mary Ann Hoberman

The True Story of the Three Little Pigs by Jon Scieszka

Uncle Jed's Barbershop by Margaree Mitchell

The Very Busy Spider by Eric Carl

Waiting for Wings by Louis Ehlert

Whales Passing by Eve Bunting

What a Year by Tomie De Paola

You Can't Eat Your Chicken Box, Amber Brown by Paula Danziger

You Read to Me, I'll Read to You: Very Short Stories to Read

Zelda and Ivy by Laura McGee Kvasnosky

Zinnia and Dot by Lisa Ernst

Congratulations

_____

name

has completed all the exercises in
this workbook and is ready
for first grade.

_____

date